Cloaked Specters Series
A Rose Narrative

Promedy
of
Errors

S. Weary

Also available by S. Weary

Meandering the Veiled Path

ISBN: 148102244X
ISBN-13: 978-1481022446

Dedication

To all first loves lost

Acknowledgements

As always, first and foremost to God for helping me to
see the humor in the craziness that has been my life.
I want to acknowledge anyone that might have inspired
any part of this creation, without naming names of course.
That being said, this is a work of fiction and any resemblance
to any persons living or dead is by coincidence.
My gratitude to Di, Audrey, and Tana who helped me bounce
ideas around and kicked me back in gear when I was stuttering.
My thanks to KS, DL, SS, CB, MJ , SM, and TS for supplying
their descriptions of me and being both helpful and accepting
of my different approach to just about everything.
My endless appreciation to Deidre for pushing me to take the
leap in this journey and for helping me to find my courage to
put my thoughts to paper and set it all free into the world.

To my readers and fans, I thank you for your support
and hope you enjoy reading this, my first novel,
as much as I enjoyed writing it.

~ *Prologue* ~

For everyone else it's just a typical mid-February Friday in a typical small town high school, but for Lea, it's special, and it's about be even more so. As it has been whenever possible, Lea's boyfriend, John, will be picking her up after school. A ritual she's been lucky enough to enjoy more often since he quit his job after he enlisted in the military. Not entirely sure when he has to leave, she chooses not to think about it, but instead, focuses on what time she has to see him now, especially today. For you see, today is her eighteenth birthday.

She leaves her last class and puts her books back in her locker. She grabs her coat and heads towards the doors where she knows he'll be parked only to see him walking towards her with a small bouquet of shiny, Happy Birthday balloons. She smiles from ear to ear.

"I'm going to have to complain about the total embarrassment he's putting me through by bringing these silly balloons in the school for everyone to see," Raven grumbles.

"You can complain as much as you want to me. I love it! And I happen to know that you like this too, so you better not bitch so much that he stops doing stuff like this for us!" Emerald argues back.

Thistle jumps up and down almost singing, "Balloons, balloons, balloons!!! And Ginger's not home to pop them!"

When Lea reaches him, she wraps her arms around John's neck and gives him a hug and a kiss. She pulls back and goes to take the balloons from his hand.

"Raven! Is that what I think it is? You see it right?" Emerald beams with excitement.

"I see it." Raven confirms.

Anchored to the balloons is a small ring box. She looks up at John who smiles down at her.

"Open it! Open it! Open it!" Emerald has joined Thistle in jumping up and down.

Lea cracks open the box and peers at the brilliant sparkling quarter carat solitaire inside. She's speechless, and waiting for John to ask the anticipated and expected question, but he stands there quiet, just staring at her.

"Seriously? He's not going to ask? You've got to be kidding me. Shouldn't be surprised. He didn't actually ask me to last year's prom either, just assumed since we were dating that we'd go together." Raven rants.

"And we did, so?" Emerald is growing more agitated.

"What if he was dating a stupid chic who didn't know what this meant? He'd have to pop the question then."

"True, but he's not dating a stupid chic, is he? What's your real issue?"

"He's supposed to ask! That's my issue. Not just assume everything all the time. Maybe I'd like to be asked about these things as if he acknowledges that I have a choice in the matter," Raven snaps.

"Well, you do have a choice. You can say no, but you better do so now because otherwise I'm saying YES!" Emerald has had enough of the tantrum.

"Of course I'm saying yes, but is it really expecting too

much to want to be asked?" Raven tosses in.

"No, it's not, but that's not the way John does things, and he's still waiting on an answer." With this Emerald ends the argument.

Lea takes the ring out, puts it on her finger, looks up at John and says, "Yes," then she kisses him again. "I've got to go show Allie!" With this Lea grabs his hand and scurries up the stairs. Allie's mother is a teacher at the school, and her classroom is the best place to start looking.

Lea looks at the sparkly diamond on her finger again.

"It'll have to be sized. It's too big." Emerald observes.

"Notice anything else?" Raven inquires.

"Like?"

"Oh, I don't know. Like the fact that it's round?"

"So?"

"So....? So, didn't we go shopping for this? So, didn't I pick out what I liked? So, didn't I make sure to get it written down? So, didn't I give it to him? So, wasn't I clear in that I wanted a princess cut, square, diamond with trillions, triangles, on the sides? So, didn't I say the last thing I wanted was round anything? And it's round!"

"It's pretty and John gave it to me, so I don't care."

"Figures…" Raven shakes her head from side to side in defeat.

They reach the classroom and find Allie inside. Lea rushes over and flashes her hand. Allie looks at Lea and then at John, "Is it real?"

Lea's face drops as she takes the focus from her ring to her friend's face. "Of course… I think. I didn't ask." She turns to face John.

Allie waits until she's sure Lea can't see her and flashes her fun-loving, snarky, shit starter grin at John.

"Really? What's your name again?" John and Allie

were always relishing their little digs on each other. He turns back to Lea, who is still staring at him wide-eyed, waiting on the answer, and in the softer tone he reserved just for her, "Yes, Honey, it's real."

~ This Is Not Happening ~

It was supposed to be the happiest time of her life. Everything was going well again. The scary parts seemed over and the future was supposed to be this bright, grand adventure, but those are stories for another time.

I am the narrator of this little tale, the little fairy in her head that gets to enjoy the amusement of what's about to happen, the one that will remind her of it years down the road and help her to laugh at it. You may call me Rose.

Please, feel free to grab a drink, a snack and make yourself comfortable. I might recommend a bathroom break as well. You wouldn't want to miss anything. The fun part about getting to be an audience with me, within her head, is that you get the inside scoop, the odd conversations with herself, the comments she shouldn't, and doesn't, say out loud, and the full color image of her warped teenage perceptions. We all know how firmly based in reality teenagers are.

Let me bring you up to speed. This young lady before you is Leanna. She's a very informal girl both in and out of her head, so everyone just calls her Lea. She's a senior, good student, good daughter, youngest child, very few close friends, but several friendly acquaintances. They never get to see the view you're about to get, the view from inside, and it will take decades to get her to let me release the locks.

She's of medium height with camouflage hazel eyes and brunette hair with natural copper and gold highlights. She has a larger than usual frame but is slender with an hourglass figure that she keeps hidden under baggie shirts. She really is prettier than she gives herself credit for as she barely considers herself average, never acknowledging the true attributes she has going for her, including a very pleasant smile that she doesn't show enough. She loves animals, poetry, music, and John Paulson.

John's a year older, tall, kind hearted, with sweet, warm eyes like melted chocolate. He has a firm work ethic and strong roots grounded in responsibility and family.

Music has played a huge role in Lea's life. It's how she met John, where she goes to escape the world when she needs to hide and reboot, and it's entangled her in dramas she'll be happy to leave far behind her when she graduates.

Lea met John in band. He was percussion. It wasn't the smoothest of hook ups, but it was worth the stumbles. She had to pursue him, and there seemed to be unwritten rules as to who was acceptable for the percussion to date, usually anyone from the rifle squad, and certain others if they were cool enough. Lea was part of the brass and miles away from making that list. Lea didn't consider herself on the same planet as some of those girls, but John was so sweet, so she didn't give up.

The first time he asked her to be his girlfriend she didn't hear him clearly and said no. She tried to back pedal and fix it, but that didn't work, so she had to keep trying.

They were hanging out at his house the day after graduation of his junior year, effectively making him a senior. They were snuggled on his parents' couch, watching TV, when John took her class ring off her finger, slid it halfway up his pinky, and replaced it with his own, which was huge on her and circled her finger wildly.

Lea thought of what her father had told her when he purchased her ring for her less than six months prior. "This is for you. You are not to give it to some boy. Do you understand me?" Lea understood very well, but she wasn't about to give John the wrong impression by taking it back. Better to let her Dad get mad at her and tell John about it later, than have him misunderstand and think she's rejecting him. Better yet, if her Dad says something in front of John, he'll know she's not just making it up. It'll be worth getting yelled at.

She looked up at John. "Are you sure?" She knew that by choosing her publicly there would be a backlash with some of his friends in the drum line. She wasn't exactly labeled a prize catch by anyone, more like an unpolished gem washed up on the shores of the island for misfit girlfriends.

"I'm a senior. It's my last year. What do I care what anyone says?" John may have thought that was supposed to be reassuring, and, if Lea had any other prospects, she might have been more insulted by that decree. It was neither reassuring nor insulting, but it was a beginning.

That was over a year and a half ago. For the first year, while he was still in school with her, they were virtually inseparable. He would pick her up and drop her off every day. He'd wait if she had swim practice or dance choir. She hung around if the drum line had an extra rehearsal. They'd steal kisses between classes, held hands whenever they could, and spent every spare second their parents would allow together. Lea's mom got sick that spring and had surgery, and Lea spent spring break in the hospital not sure exactly what was causing her pain and issues, but John was still there with her as much as he could be.

Of course all that changed when John graduated. He got a job. Lea's mom began chemotherapy and radiation. She cut her hair super short when it started falling out by the handful because it was less traumatic and ended up with nothing but white stubble left. Lea got a summer job but had to quit before the season ended when she had to have surgery herself to remove a cyst that was threatening her life. By fall, Lea was back in school and busy with activities; John was still working and now going to the local college; and Lea's mom was having severe adverse reactions to her treatments.

That fall was hard on Lea and would alter her in ways she wouldn't realize for years to come. She was alone most of the time. Her parent's conceded to let her get her driver's license since John was no longer able to get her to and from school and Lea's Mom was too weak most of the time to keep up with the demanding schedule anymore.

Ultimately Lea's mom would end up in a coma for a week. For the first three days, the family was told not to expect her to survive. She would be in the hospital for almost a month and even when she did come home, both Lea and her mother lived with the fear that one morning Lea would wake up to find her mother dead, but they never spoke of that, hoping the other wasn't thinking it and trying to save each other from that kind of worry.

Fall passed, Christmas came and John announced to everyone that he had enlisted in the military. He hadn't done badly his first semester. He just thought this would be a better career choice in the long run. All Lea could hear was that he was leaving. At least he was also going to be quitting his job soon so she'd get to see him more often before he left. John took her shopping at the jewelry store to see what she would want after he started getting paid and could afford it.

Of course, he preferred to make sure she didn't change her mind or forget about him and surprised her on her birthday before reminding her that he would be leaving in four days for basic training.

A dark figure emerges from the shadows cloaked in textured, ebony velvet and obscured in a large black satin hood edged with raven feathers. The voice that resounds is a little harsher than anticipated, a little deeper, and with more edge than eighteen years should have tainted. This shadow is stronger than it should be in that time. "I bet you got a wonderful little chuckle out of that moment. Didn't you, Rose?" With this, the cloaked figure recesses to a blood red settee in the corner, returning the floor to Rose.

Lea and John had been in a car accident the year prior, and Lea had received a small settlement. She takes it as a good sign as it would cover the cost of tickets for her Prom. No need to ask Dad for it. John assures her that he will be able to come back to take her. No need to fear. All is well. She buys the tickets, planning to go with her fiancé. She continues towards the vision painted in her head to make this the night of her dreams.

The next challenge is to negotiate the attendance of her best friend, Allie, who otherwise won't be able to go. It is for juniors, seniors, and their invited guests only, and, since Allie is only a freshman, something has to be done or it won't be a perfect night. By a stroke of luck, there is a senior that has a crush on Allie and still no date. Allie grumbles a little about how she doesn't like him that way.

Raven rises again to chime in, "But that doesn't matter because this is my Prom, my plan, and it will be perfect! It only took a little whispering in Carl's ear to get him to ask Allie, and I warned her that saying no is not an option, not if she really considers herself my best friend, not after all I've been through, not unless she single handedly wants to ruin my Senior Prom." The black cloak grumbles and dismisses herself back into the shadows.

Lea has a gift for guilt trips and manipulation. I believe it's hereditary. It also makes me wonder if her toddler tantrums played out in similar fashion.

The time passes slowly. *It doesn't feel right with John gone. She's lost.* With these words, the cloaked figure shifts in her chair. *She waits for letters and calls, which are not as frequent as she would like. These are stolen moments within a balloon where she can pretend that the world will play out according to her hopes. Until... the phone rings.*

"Hello?" Lea answers.

"Is Lea home?" John's voice reaches across the lines and lights her up like a Christmas tree.

"It's me." Lea's voice mellows, and she walks to her parent's bedroom where she can take the call with some privacy.

"Hey, Honey. How are you?"

"Not bad, much better now that you've called. How are you holding up?"

"Getting through."

"I miss you."

"Miss you too."

"So I got Allie a date for Prom."

"Who?"

"Carl."

"Why Carl?"

"I thought it might be nice if you had someone to talk

to and, since you both were on the line together, it made sense. Besides, he's got a crush on her. She keeps catching him staring at her during band. She thinks it's a little creepy and wasn't overly thrilled with the idea, but me being the wonderfully persuasive person I am, convinced her of all the benefits of the arrangement."

"What did you threaten her with?"

"I didn't have to threaten her at all… I just pouted a little when she started whining about it and reminded her that she was supposed to be my best friend and how hard it was that first night when I found out Mom was in a coma and I couldn't find her… and that's about when she caved in and said fine."

"Yeah, your wonderfully persuasive self. Hey, my time's almost up. I'll be home in a week. We'll talk more about this then. I can't wait to see you."

"Me either. Don't forget we have an appointment for pictures while you're here."

"I know. I got your letter about that. I've gotta run."

"I love you."

"Love you, too."

Click.

A new figure appears, also hidden from full view by a cloak, emerald green with intricate lime accents embroidered on it, the hood a lime satin with emerald edging. The figure exudes a growth and life of its own. Her voice sings a lighter more innocent song as she speaks.

"It's always so nice to hear from him," Emerald floats to the farthest corner from where Raven is perched to find a dainty vined chaise awaiting her.

"Gushy nonsense…," Raven mumbles. "I can't stand it when you're like this."

"Whatever… Get used to it. I'm counting the days."

Emerald swirls and twirls her robes.

The week passes quickly, and John arrives as planned. Lea's surprised at how he's changed. His hair is cut short; he's lost weight; and his face is thinned out. He looks so much more grown up than when he left eight weeks ago, and he's handsome in a way she didn't previously notice.

His time is spread thin with visits to as many of his family as he can. Lea's days are still occupied with school, allowing them only an hour or two to see each other on any given day.

Their photo appointment is the following Friday, and John picks her up in his uniform. He's not thrilled about wearing it, but at least it's only his working blues, which are actually just black pants, a black button up shirt, and a black tie, which he chooses not to wear. It was the only way to get him to wear it at all, but even incomplete, John looks better than Lea has ever seen him look before. Lea has thrown together a red jacket and slacks combo with a black top underneath.

They get through their appointment quickly and grab something to eat. Lea eats her fill and then slides her food aside.

"So what will it take for me to get you to wear that to Prom?" Lea beams as she stares at him.

"About that..." John looks away momentarily, trying to find the words.

Lea notices the shift in mood and tone, her expression one of confusion.

John reaches his hand across the table. "I'm not going to be able to come back for Prom. I can't do both Prom and graduation, and I really want to be here when you graduate."

Lea looks down at his hand holding hers and the ring

he gave to her, "Oh, I see."

"*Difference between girls and guys. Girls would know to choose Prom instead.*" *Raven glowers and grumbles.*

Lea does her best to blink away the tears welling up in her eyes before looking back up at John.

"I'm sorry," he croons at her.

"It's fine," she lies. "It's just another stupid dance anyway. We went last year. No big deal. We should get going, I didn't tell anyone we were going anywhere after the pictures." Lea stands quickly, pulling her hand away, and heads to the bathroom. She wipes her face free of tears and resets her composure before heading back out to join John.

"You okay?" John asks when they are alone in the car.

"I'm fine," Lea lies again, but more convincingly this time. John grabs her hand, but the ride home is completely silent.

Framework appears around Raven's nook with a half gazebo design, encompassing her.

"*Raven, what are you doing?*" *Emerald is truly concerned by what she's watching transpire.* "*I thought we put this away after Mom woke up last fall.*"

"*We did, but things have changed since then, haven't they?*" *Raven answers.*

"*You don't need walls around you,*" *Emerald urges.*

"*You have no idea what I need, and they're far from complete. We serve different purposes, Emerald.*"

"*But you aren't the only one that will be affected by this.*"

"*Don't you think I know that? I'm doing the best I can.*" *Raven walks around the perimeter. As she passes, the empty frame fills with waist high half walls, leaving an open archway for her to walk through.*

Emerald starts working overtime trying to find a bright side to this news, "*This is not the end of the world. Allie is going with Carl. Allie's never been considered a third wheel with John and I. I won't be a third wheel with them. We have a full table of fun people, and we'll still have a good time. I'm not thrilled about having to go by myself, but I can deal with this. Besides, it's probably better this way. If we hadn't already gotten Allie a date, I might have considered letting her go with me and hang out, but it's nineteen ninety, and this is rural, bible belt, Midwest, so that might not be taken so well. It might be considered too much of a lesbian outreach for their taste, even though the whole world, meaning our little town, knows I'm engaged.*

"Now I just need to go tell Mom that I'm going stag and ask if I can borrow the car that night. I know it's an hour away, and, of course, I wasn't planning on having to drive, but it'll be fine. She'll make sure Dad's cool with this."

John pulls into the driveway, but Lea doesn't wait for him to shut off the car and walk her in. She leans over, gives him a kiss, jumps out of the car, and swiftly walks into the house. Unsure what she's expecting of him, he hesitates before following her inside.

With Emerald's declaration of purpose still ringing in her head, off Lea goes to find her mother and break the news, full of confidence and a complete refusal to implode over this. It's just a snag. There's a long life ahead with John. Besides, she went with him to his senior prom last year. True, this year was supposed to be for her, no snide comments from her friend's date in a bellboy tux saying her dress looked 'waterproof,' but that isn't the point. It'll be fine.

Lea finds her mother at the dining table, sewing together her prom dress, a Marilyn Monroe *Seven Year Itch* inspired peach frock, minus the pleats in the skirt and with a plunging, but not overly revealing, V in both the front and back, to appease the modesty of Lea, her father, and their geographical locale. The waist is a black, pressed velvet design that flowed, twisted, and meandered with a copper-gold background peeking through, with accents of the black down the sides of the skirt and along the neckline.

"Don't go anywhere. I'm going to want you to try this on in just a couple minutes," her mother says as she walks up. "How'd the appointment go?" Lea's mother glances up realizing Lea is alone. "Where's John?"

"Actually I need to talk to you." Her voice is not as solid and sure as she was hoping it'd be, but she continues, "John's not going to be able to make it back for Prom, so I'm going solo."

Lea's mother looks up at her. John comes to stand behind Lea. "You won't be back, John?"

"I can't, but I'm planning on being here for graduation," John answers. The disappointment on her mom's face is evident, but John adds, "Is it okay if I steal Lea away for the next couple days? I fly out Sunday afternoon, and I'd like to spend as much time with her as I can before I go."

"What did you have in mind?"

"Well, I was thinking movies at my house tonight, and my family is having a big gathering for me tomorrow at my aunt's place, mostly games and hanging around kinda thing. I'll bring her back tonight and pick her up early tomorrow if that's okay with you."

"Sure, not a problem. Lea, we can talk about this after he leaves." She removes the dress from the machine, extending it towards her daughter. "Just hang this up for now. You can try it on later, and hurry up and change. You don't want the cat getting fur all over John's uniform. The longer you take, the fuzzier he's going to end up."

Lea does as she's told, and, although John has dealt

her a deeply saddening blow, she does her best to enjoy their waning time together before he leaves again. They go over to his house and spend the evening in his room.

It's small, but he's done his best to make the most of the space, considering his queen sized water bed is centered on the back wall leaving little room for anything else except the nightstand on the left side. There's less than five feet from the foot of the bed to the closet, which also conceals his television and video equipment. There's just enough space between the bottom edge of the bed and the door frame for his tall stereo system, and his dresser is directly across from the door between his closet and window. The carpet is dark brown and the walls have wood paneling below the chair rail and a nondescript beige paint above. He has a few posters on the walls of bands with renowned drummers.

The rules are well understood, and they leave the door cracked open only slightly, giving his parents' the possibility of walking in at any time, thusly assuring proper limits must be maintained, but it also allows them some privacy for making out.

Lea curls up next to him on his bed. She doesn't care what movie he puts in and pays very little attention to it, choosing instead to cuddle as closely to him as she can get away with, trying to make the moment last, trying to pretend she doesn't have to go home, trying to cling to him with all the desperation she's feeling inside but can't put into words.

By the time John takes her home, Lea's mom is already asleep. She puts on pajamas, curls up in her bed, and cries herself to sleep.

Lea's mom wakes her in the morning and tells her John is already there to pick her up. Lea jumps out of bed and rushes through a shower, washing, drying, and getting herself dressed in jeans and a baggy paisley print button up, all in less than fifteen minutes. She unwraps the towel from around her head, yanks a brush through it quickly, fluffs it back up with her fingers, grabs her makeup bag and hurries out to the living room, hair still very damp.

John is sitting on the couch petting Lea's cat that has perched on his lap. He's in his usual wardrobe of jeans, sneakers, t-shirt, jean jacket, and baseball cap.

"I'm sorry. I must have turned the alarm clock off in my sleep." Lea apologizes.

"It's fine. I came by early, just in case. Ready?"

"Yeah, I can finish in the car." Lea slips on her black flats that she'd left by the couch the night before and grabs her purse.

Lea's cat is perturbed when John slides her over setting her next to him so he can stand up. He follows Lea out the door, paying the animal no further attention.

Lea slaps on some makeup while John drives. The house is full of aunts, uncles, cousins, spouses, girlfriends, and children. His parents are already there. John's dad is in the front room with the other men discussing manly things. His mom is in the dining room with two of his aunts and a couple cousins playing cards. The rest of the brood is milling around eating or in the family room setting up board games on the card tables.

Lea follows John as he makes his rounds, being greeted and hugged and told how proud everyone is and how much they've missed him. She gets hugged frequently and told she shouldn't be such a stranger while he's gone. Lea stays close to John, holding his hand like a tether of safety whenever she can. She does her best to fit into the crowd, but always feels a little unbalanced and overwhelmed.

Raven backs into her alcove. Emerald tries to coax her back out, "Come back out here. What's the matter?"

"I'm not used to this." Raven waves her off. "They're so close and nice to each other, nice to me. You know I don't know how to process this, having a family that actually enjoys spending time together and is loving and caring instead of snippy and insulting. This is all yours. I'm just gonna hang back here."

"This is great! You're missing out." Emerald revels in the moments with John's family.

After the required initial circulation, they head back to the kitchen to grab something to eat. The potluck buffet has a little of everything. John's family has a wonderful ability to cooperate together for the betterment of everyone. In all of the gatherings like this that John has brought Lea along to, she's never once witnessed any drama or discord.

She's too unsure and prefers to stay close to John the entire time they're there. They join in a couple games. Lea, who is normally very competitive, never wins but also doesn't mind. She enjoys the fun for fun's sake. The time flies. Before she realizes it, several hours have past and people are beginning to clear out.

John's mother comes in to let him know that it's time to go. His dad already has his coat on and is heading out to start their car. John and Lea make the rounds again saying goodbyes, everyone hugging or shaking his hand as they try to leave. Lea secretly holds the back hem of his jacket whenever she's not being hugged herself.

John opens Lea's door for her, and she drops in. He climbs behind the wheel and grabs her hand the moment the car is in gear. They pull away, heading into town instead of back towards Lea's house.

"Where are we going?" she wonders out loud.

"My parents are taking us to dinner," John answers.

"Did you tell my mom about this?"

"Sure did."

"When exactly were you planning to tell me? I could have dressed better."

"You look fine," John lifts her hand and kisses it. "Besides, I didn't think it mattered too much since I'm your ride. You're kind of stuck with me until I decide to take you home."

"And when will that be?"

"Never."

"I'm okay with that, but my parents might freak out." Lea rests her head on his shoulder, holding his hand with both of hers on her lap.

"Well I wasn't given an actual time to get you back, so I think we have some leeway tonight as long as I don't keep you 'til morning."

"That's a shame. That couldn't have been interesting."

"Especially with my parents on the other side of my bedroom wall."

"That is kind of a drawback to your bed. It's warm and comfy, but too noisy."

"Wasn't really an issue before you came along."

"I'm sorry."

"Don't be. I'm not."

Lea leans up and kisses John's neck. He tenses next to her.

"Do you have to start that now?" He asks, not really wanting her to stop.

"Yes, I do." Lea smiles wickedly and kisses and nibbles his neck some more. "And if you're lucky, I'll continue it later too."

John moans quietly. "You know you're making it difficult to drive."

"I would have thought you'd be used to it by now. This car is the only place we ever get to be alone."

"Yeah, but it's been awhile."

"I know…"

John releases Lea's hand and grabs her thigh halfway above her knee and squeezes gently. He stops at a red light and turns to kiss her, searing her lips with his own and sending tingles cascading across her entire body. He pulls away to check the light just as it changes. Lea leans her head back on his shoulder and rests her hand on top of his.

They arrive at the restaurant shortly after his parents, who are still waiting to be seated. Dinner is pleasant, as usual when dining with his family. Lea is more comfortable when it's just the three or four of them, depending on if his father is able to join them due to his work shift.

John's parents are caring and kind to each other, to their son, and to Lea, and they have been since the beginning. She's never seen them raise their voices in anger towards each other, not once. Lea knows it's not just an act for her benefit because of John's reaction when he witnessed firsthand how her parents could yell at each other, and they weren't even arguing that time. John cried.

Lea's grown used to the 'he who yells loudest gets heard' environment. She started yelling back when she was thirteen, but she doesn't have to yell around John. She gets to enjoy the quiet moments of life when she's with him.

"You know he deserves somebody better than me, don't you, Emerald?" Raven evaluates.

"Yes, but he chose me, so is it really fair for me to second guess that?" Emerald replies. "Besides, are you ignoring how happy I am when I'm with him?"

"I'm not ignoring anything. I also know how much it's hurt since he left, how amazing his family is, how dysfunctional

mine is in comparison, and how damaged I am."

"He doesn't see me as damaged."

"I know. I can't decide if he's blind or just choosing to ignore it because he doesn't want to see it."

"I don't care. I love him, and he loves me. That's good enough for me." Emerald puts an end to their exchange.

After dinner, the couples split ways in the parking lot, both heading back to the Paulson home. Lea squirms uncomfortably in her seat in John's car, weighing the truth of Raven's words against the tight bonds of John's extended family, the battlefield her home can turn into against the safe, peaceful calm she feels at his.

John squeezes her hand, "Honey, what's wrong?"

"Nothing," she mutters.

"Yes, there is. What it is?"

"Lots of things."

"Prom?"

"Partly, and you're leaving tomorrow. It feels like you just got home, and you're leaving again."

"I know it does."

Lea sniffles and fights back the tears welling in her eyes.

"What else is bothering you?"

"You have no idea how much I need you or how you've crushed me by leaving me behind," Raven interjects.

"Raven, don't. He can't know how pathetically weak I really am. I can't lose him," Emerald pleads.

"Nothing," Lea hides her insecurities and fear.

His parents are already home when he pulls his car next to the garage. Lea pats her eyes before reaching for the handle to get out. John's waiting by her door. He presses his full soft lips gingerly against hers before leading her inside.

His parents are settling in their living room. His

father, being a strong preparation and responsibilities first type, asks if John's packed yet, wanting to make sure tomorrow won't be chaotic and rushed. Lea excuses herself to the bathroom, leaving them to their conversation.

When she steps back out, John is already across the hall in his room. He hears the door and turns to face her. She looks towards the living room and back towards John, not sure where she should go.

"It's his last night here. It'd be selfish of me if we just hide away in his room all night," Emerald confesses.

"Exactly. It's his last night here, and we've had very little privacy the whole time he's been back," Raven debates.

John smiles at her and waves her in.

"Aren't they expecting us out there with them?" Lea asks him.

"No, and for the next few hours, I just want to be with you." John kisses her again, temporarily wiping Lea's mind of everything else.

"Okay," Lea hums up at him.

"Get comfortable. Mom wants to wash this stuff before I go," John pulls on his shirt. "I'll be right back." He grabs a pair of shorts and a t-shirt from his dresser and leaves the room.

Lea takes off her shoes and is laid out on his bed when he returns. He closes the door, but doesn't let it latch.

"Isn't that supposed to be cracked open?" she reminds him.

"It's not technically closed. And what are they going to do? Ground me?"

"Call my parents and get me grounded…"

John crawls onto the bed next to her, "No, they won't. Did Dad rat us out when he walked in on us that time in the living room before Mom got home? No."

"True, but you know my parents."

"Yeah, but we're not at your house, and my parents see it a little differently." John runs his hand over her waist, pulling his body close to hers.

"Really? How do they see it?" Lea smiles, her eyes flirtatious and encouraging.

"We're both adults."

"I'm still in high school."

"But I'm not, and you're over eighteen, and we're engaged to be married," John stifles her ability to counter his argument by kissing her.

He lifts away and Lea starts to make her delayed point, "But…" John hushes her a second time with his kisses, not stopping until he's sure he's put an end to any further protests.

He looks down at her grinning, "You were saying?"

"Huh?"

"Nothing," he leans over and begins kissing her again.

Lea's mouth burns, his kisses setting seismic ripples of heat shooting through her. John's hand slides just under her shirt and electric currents shoot across her where their skin connects. Her mind swirls with a wanton craving she's only ever known from his touch.

John pulls away, rolling on his back. Lea catches her breath and curls up on her side, keeping her body against his. She places her leg over and between his and rests her head on his shoulder, nuzzling into his neck. She wraps her arm over him and squeezes him, hugging herself tightly to him. He rests his available hand on her arm and returns her embrace, kissing the top of her head.

They lie there watching tv, Lea refusing to release him, wanting to hold him as long and as close as she can.

She listens to his heart beat and lets her hand drift back and forth across his chest, over his shirt.

Emerald is seated on her ornately vined bench weeping softly, "I don't want him to go."

Raven sits next to her, opening her arms and letting her companion lean against her, "I know."

"I'm so comfortable here, so much more relaxed. I wish we had more time like this," Emerald adds.

Raven teeters them back and forth, "I know, I know. Hush now. Try not to think about it. There'll be time for that tomorrow. Just enjoy this now."

A tear slides out of the corner of Lea's eye. She doesn't want to waste his last night having him watch her cry. She lifts her face to his neck, fluttering light kisses against his warm skin. John closes his eyes and there's a skitter in his breath.

"John," his mother calls seconds before opening his door. Lea stops, retreating her leg next to his instead of over it and setting her head back on his shoulder innocently.

"Yeah," he answers without moving or letting Lea go.

His mother stands in the door, "Was there anything else you needed washed tonight?"

"Nope, that was it."

Lea keeps her eyes on the television, not wanting to see the look on his mother's face, but still wondering what the wonderful woman must think of her and how she's positioned in her son's bed.

"Okay. Don't fall asleep. You still have to take her home sometime tonight," she reminds him.

John reassures her, "I'll set the alarm." Lea moves so he can roll over and set his clock.

With that, John's mom turns and leaves, closing the door completely behind her.

John turns back towards Lea, "I need a drink, and, if you start up like that again, I'm not going to want to go get it. You want one?"

"Yes, please."

He gives her a peck on the lips and walks out. Gulping down a soda when he returns, John closes the door completely, hands a can over to Lea, and puts his on the nightstand. He waits until Lea has opened her can and is taking a drink before shutting off the lights and returning to his bed next to her. He takes her can from her, placing it next to his own.

"Where were we?" John asks as he wraps his arm around her again and pulls her leg back over him with his other hand.

"And what if your mother comes back?" Lea asks not fighting him.

"Doubt that'll happen."

"How can you be so sure?" she cuddles back into him, breathing her words on his neck.

"Because she just told me she'd leave my clothes folded on the dining room table when they were done, and I suspect she'll be going to bed after that."

"And your dad?" Lea starts kissing his neck again.

"How often has he walked in here?"

"Well he caught us once already."

"In the middle of the living room floor..."

Lea nibbles on his ear and whispers, "if you're sure..." She moves her hand under his shirt, needing to feel his skin against her fingers.

John groans minutely. He grabs her leg and pulls her on top of him, kissing her wildly, his hands unbuttoning her shirt. He reaches around to unfasten her bra.

Lea chuckles at him breaking their lip lock.

"What the?" he mumbles, flustered.

Lea sits up, straddling him, "Front clasp."

"That's a new one."

Even in the shadowed flashes from the television, she can tell he's smiling, "Wishful thinking," she admits, reaching up and releasing it.

He runs his hands up the sides of her body, then continues exploring her, driving her crazy. She pushes his shirt up exposing his chest and then lays back down, pressing herself against him. He wraps his arms around her, under her shirt, and kisses her again, letting his hands rub up and down her back and over her hips. Her body flushes and burns from the inside out.

They hear footsteps in the hall and Lea hurriedly slides off of him. The bed sloshes beneath them as she returns to their cuddled position. She pulls her shirt together and John yanks his down in case his door opens again. She snickers, slightly embarrassed by the rush she feels at the risk of almost getting caught again.

John reaches for his nightstand. He grabs her soda first and passes it to her, then reaches back for his own. He swallows down a long drink and puts it back, waiting for Lea to finish before taking hers and replaces it as well.

"I think that was Mom heading to the bedroom," John says quietly.

"What time is it?" she asks.

John looks at his alarm, "Nine."

"And she's going to bed this early?"

"She's probably watching some tv first."

"But your dad's probably gonna be up 'til after you have to take me home."

"Yeah, but he's at the other end of the house, and I plan on keeping you here."

Lea teases him, "But what if I tried to leave?"

She halfheartedly starts to lift away from him, only to have him roll over her, letting his presence push her back down.

"If that's what you really wanna do…" John kisses her again.

She melts into the moment with him, lifting his shirt off and pulling him back down on her. She wraps her legs around him and grips onto him for dear life.

They spend the better part of the next couple hours lost in each other, kissing, touching, and trying to be connected in every way possible, without violating Lea's personal code. John never pushes her farther than she's comfortable going and never complains about her limit.

"I know you don't really want to stop, Emerald," Raven barks her frustration.

"That doesn't matter. You know as well as I do what Mom said about our family," Emerald breathes back heavily.

"Yeah, yeah, I know. 'Don't have sex or you'll get pregnant'," Raven seethes.

"Not yet. I don't want everyone thinking he's marrying me because he knocked me up. I don't want them all thinking that the only reason he's with me is because I was easy and put out," Emerald takes her stand.

"Why do you care what they think anyway? Let John move you away from here, put it all behind you, and never look back," Raven bellows.

"You're the one ranting about how I'm not good enough for him. Maybe this is about me! If I'm going to believe that I am, then I need to know that he respects me enough to wait for me to be at a point that I won't regret it." Emerald squares her shoulders and lifts her chin.

"Fine, but I hope you don't end up regretting passing up

these opportunities that you've had with him and may or may not get again," Raven withdrawals.

"I'd rather regret passing up an opportunity than actively doing something contrary to my beliefs," Emerald spouts idealistically.

"Funny. I'd rather regret living and doing than waiting for some perfect moment in life that might never happen," Raven turns away conceding the point she knows she won't win tonight.

They hear footsteps again, forcing them back into a composed state. John quickly grabs his shirt and puts it back on. Lea rolls on her stomach hiding the fact that she's still completely exposed from the waist up, resting her face on his arm. There's a light knock at his door.

Lea stuffs the edges of her shirt under her and closes her eyes.

"Yeah?" John answers.

John's dad opens the door and turns on the light. "What time does she need to be home?"

John looks at Lea and then his clock, "I set the alarm to go off in about a half hour, so I'll wake her up then and take her home."

"Okay," his dad shuts the light back off, steps out, and closes the door.

Lea raises her head and rolls over, redressing herself. She grabs John's hand and rolls away from him, directing him to spoon behind her. She yawns and wiggles back against him, not caring how short her nap might be, knowing it'll be worth it just to fall asleep in his arms. He surrounds her with warmth, and she drifts off.

John's alarm goes off and he wakes her with soft kisses behind her ear. "Time to go," he whispers sweetly.

He climbs out of bed and throws on a pair of sweat pants over his shorts and grabs his shoes. Groggy, Lea works her way down to the foot of the bed and puts on her shoes.

John's dad is still in the family room when they pass through on the way to John's car.

"Thank you for dinner. Good night." Lea waves as she steps out the door.

"You're welcome. Night," He nods his head and then turns towards John, "Drive careful."

"I will," John follows Lea out.

The drive home is quiet. Lea doesn't want to think about how long it will be before she can see him again. He walks her inside and gives her another series of kisses good bye.

"Call me tomorrow so I know you got there safe," Lea's voice cracks betraying her true emotions.

"I will," John kisses her deeply once more. He walks out to his car and drives away.

Lea heads to bed and sobs into her pillow.

Sunday, she finds her mother double checking her work on the dress. "I've thought about what you said, and I am not going through all this trouble so you can go by yourself. You can't go stag. It's just not done, not by girls. You paid for two tickets, and I won't sit by and let you waste the money like that. You will be using both tickets. You can take your sister, Ginger." She extends the dress to Lea for her to try on.

Externally, Lea stands frozen, a stone statue of utter disbelief. Internally, both cloaked figures jump to their feet. Emerald gasps in horror, while Raven growls through clenched teeth, "This. Is. Not. Happening."

~ *Yes It Is* ~

Lea takes the dress and heads to the bathroom to try it on.

Both Emerald and Raven start pacing in front of their seats. Their hoods shake from side to side, their agitation seeping through their cloaks. Rose watches but decides that attempting to calm them is a complete waste of her time.

This might seem like a complete overreaction, but you don't understand the players. You've already met Mother, the vacuous kewpie doll... blink, blink, blink.

Raven rejoins the moment. "She used to be generally dependable and creative with only slightly annoying tendencies to be flighty and submissive with Cleaver family delusions."

Emerald stops her pacing and snaps back, "Be nice! She's been through a lot, and she's lucky to even be here. It's not her fault that she's now taking a smoothie mixed from the drain sink of a pharmaceutical lab on a daily basis, or that her brain was spun on liquefy during those seizures. Have you forgotten she checked out for a week? You could be a little nicer."

"She's gone too far this time, and you know it," Raven

huffs. "You don't want me popping off about this. Fine, but what are you going to do about it?"

Emerald sags as if her robe was now lined with lead. "I don't know. Let me think," her voice hushed. They both return to their pacing with only slightly less agitation.

Beyond her ever complicated mother, Lea also lives with her father, a loving, if emotionally distant, blue-collar worker and her two sisters, Vikki and Ginger, in a moderate ranch house, with a reasonable yard in a line of similar, rural, ranch homes. It has four bedrooms, but shares one bath, which made life interesting when there were three teenage girls and Mom all trying to get ready at the same time. There's a large living room and a combination kitchen and dining room that has a good sized table that they use for sewing, crafting, and whatever else they may need beyond the special occasion meals.

Vikki is quiet and nice. She's the dependable, hard-working one. She's not one to argue back on anything. Her favorite word is "Whatever". She's not unattractive, but, given her competition, she isn't often noticed for all the attributes she has to offer. It's probably a more appealing option for her to meet guys when she is out with her friends and never bring them home to meet the family.

Mother was once asked who she would want with her if she was stranded on a deserted island. She replied that it would be Vikki because she works so well with her.

"Yeah, boat sinks and make sure Vikki makes it. She never mouths off, never speaks her opinion, never calls anyone out on anything when they might be wrong." The sarcasm drips from Raven as she speaks. "Leave us to the sharks, or to drown, but save the silent, dutiful one."

Emerald can't restrain herself from adding her own tidbit, "Notice she wasn't asked who was her favorite, who was the golden child."

Rose clears her throat to try to reclaim the floor, but Raven isn't ready to relinquish it just yet.

"Ah yes, the golden child, Ginger, the pigmy love child of Aphrodite and Aries with a hidden side that KewpieMom never sees. It's amazing how big a shadow is cast from her five foot one, less than a hundred pound frame. It's not that I never see the sunlight. I mean, I am quite noticeably taller than she is. It's just that it's usually in the form of the rare glimpse that is reflected off her long, golden tresses." Raven's bitterness is surprising. "Plus, her genetically engineered cheekbones and big, blue, slanting cat's eyes that distract from the barbed tongue and secret geyser of aggression that can propel a punch so hard I can't move my arm for three days, yet it simmers unnoticed until she can unleash it without risk of getting into trouble."

Emerald chokes out through quiet tears, "she's so talented. I've admired her for so long, wanted guys to notice me like they did her, wished I could be like her, and longed to get her approval of anything I ever did….."

Rose helps her to her seat as Raven continues again. "And what did she offer in return for all my admiration? She treats me like an unwanted stray dog that keeps hanging around no matter how many times she kicks it. The one compliment she ever gave me was to compare me to a corpse."

Rose rises and looks at Lea's reflection. Lea has on the dress. It looks lovely enough, but it's as if she now sees it through a frosted film, unable to be as excited as she was when she first envisioned all these preparations weeks ago, her moment dimmed and fading by the dread of what may be to come.

"I've got it!!!" Emerald exclaims. "If I can get someone else to go with me, then I won't have to take the demonic imp. I just have to find a date."

With renewed hope and relief, Lea walks back out to

show Mother and propose a new solution. She stands and twirls in front of Mother, finding a grin to show her gratitude for all the labored work that has been put into the garment despite Mother's still weakened state, and trying her best to disguise the anxiety, panic, and horror that still hovers just beneath the surface.

Lea's voice sounds tentative and polite, "Mom… if I can find a friend to go with me instead, is it okay if I don't go with Ginger?"

"Please say yes, please say yes, please say yes,… ," Emerald pleas, prays and begs towards the woman who can't see her and has no idea the torment she has released at the mere proposition of her words. Raven too sits on the edge of her seat, tense and watchful.

"That'd be fine. As long as the other ticket gets used, and you don't go alone," Mother fidgets with the dress, taking mental note of what needs adjusting. She focuses on the fabric, completely oblivious to the animosity between her children. Maybe she thinks if they are forced to spend time together they will somehow develop the unbreakable bond of closeness that she desires for them, but that's a pipedream that's not likely to ever happen.

The cloaks take a collective sigh. There is hope once again. Allie's going. Dress is all but done. Now there's a new focus. She's still got a few weeks. Who can she ask?

Lea decides her best option is her dance partner and friend, Brian. He's newly available. He was previously dating Lea's friend, Lauren. She's tall, thin, and lovely and a total sweetheart to everyone. They broke up, so it's not like it would be a violation of friendship or anything.

Lea seeks him out first thing Monday morning, but comes across Allie first.

"So how'd John's visit go?" Allie asks excited for the

details.

"Don't ask," Lea growls, still seeking out Brian.

"What happened?" Allie's curiosity fuels her to ignore Lea's response.

Lea spies Brian and explains her new situation to both of them at the same time.

"That sucks!" Allie exclaims in shock.

"You know I'd go with you, but I already asked Lauren before we broke up. We're still friends, and we're still planning to go." Brian is so sincere and gentle as he lets Lea down.

"I thought she was dating Jason now. They aren't going together?" Lea inquires.

"Jason's working that night, and, since it was already set, he said he didn't have an issue with it." That ends the quick and easy solution.

"Oh. I didn't realize. Thanks anyway." Lea tries to be polite, despite the obvious disappointment.

"We're going to be late," Allie grabs Lea and pulling her away from Brian and off to band, their only class together.

Raven is less than thrilled with this outcome. "Peaceful and polite breakups are cool, but why can't they hate each other?"

Lea and Allie get out their instruments. "You've got almost a month. You'll find someone. I'll help you. We'll figure this out." Allie tries to comfort her friend before heading to their respective seats and ending their contact for the rest of the school day.

Lea moves on from her easy choice, trying to think of who is still available and will respect her situation and her relationship with John.

Emerald pipes up, "Mitch! Go ask Mitch! He's a blast, and you know he won't have an issue with you being engaged. You'll have so much fun with him." She almost glows with relief and excitement through her flowing façade.

That afternoon she heads out to the Logan home. Their families have been friends for years, and yet, with all the Logan boys to choose from, there's been no dating between them. Lea used to find that odd and would have considered it before John, but she also knows she isn't the one that young men notice. Mark is the same age as Lea. Scott is a couple years older, and a few years older than Scott is Mitch.

Lea holds all of them in high regard, but there's something quirky about Mitch that, despite their age difference, draws her to him.

Emerald further pleads her case as to why this is such a good idea as Lea drives up to their log home. "He's very easy to talk to, has a multi-layered sense of humor that always seems to include the potential for impropriety, and he not only listens, but understands, and he recognizes the hidden battle zone between Ginger and me, which so very few seem to see."

Still the nerves twist in Lea's stomach. Raven steps up and takes ahold of the building anxiety, "Seriously? You're going to let a pathetic, years old, childish crush stand in the way of what needs to be done? Get a grip already! He's a nice guy, makes you laugh 'til you cry, and is a gentleman. Get your butt out of this car and GO!"

Lea takes a deep breath and walks up to the door. By a stroke of luck, Mitch is the one to answer. That's the first lucky break she's gotten in a long time, no questioning looks as to why she's asking to see him if anyone else had answered. "Just the person I came to see." Lea smiles at the relief. Mitch steps out to join her on the porch, waving his arm slightly out, guiding her towards the chairs to the side and granting them some limited privacy from whoever else may be home.

"I know this is going to sound odd, but I find myself in need of a date for Prom." Mitch raises an eyebrow at this. What Lea wouldn't give to know what is running through his head at that moment. At least he doesn't start laughing at her. She continues, "John's not able to make it back, and, if I don't find a date, Mom said I have to take Ginger." With this, he lets out a snicker.

Raven pops in, "Even he sees the lunacy in Kewpie-Mom's request! How does she not get it?" With this, she shakes her hood back and forth and recedes again to her perch.

Mitch looks at Lea and smiles. Whatever joking comment he may have thought, he set it aside. "First, let me say I am extremely flattered…"

"NO!" Emerald exclaims knowing where this is heading.

"Buuutttttt…." Lea interrupts feeling the imminent rejection that was about to happen.

"But…, it's Mark's senior Prom too, and I don't want to ruin it for him. Scott's already going to be going as well, and I don't think it will be fair to Mark to have not just one, but both, of his brothers there."

"I understand. I can respect that, I guess. Thanks anyway," Lea tries to hide the utter dejection that is welling within her. She does her best to keep her head up as she heads back to her car, careful not to let her watering eyes betray her by letting a tear fall before she is safely hidden within her vehicle. She drives back home, blinking the tears away as best she can, only having to wipe away a few determined escapees.

A small lump is curled around itself between Raven and Emerald. "I'm scared," a tiny, weak voice seeps out. The thistle cloth wrapped around itself. The amethyst hood hung over the knees. "What if I don't find anyone? I don't want to miss it, but I can't go with her. I just can't." Thistle begins rocking back and forth, still wrapped around herself.

Emerald and Raven both glide to her side and kneel next to her. "It'll be okay," Emerald consoles. "I've only asked two people. I'll make a list and keep going until someone says yes."

Raven, being ever realistic and trying to convey much more confidence than she actually feels, adds, "And if it ends up being Ginger, I won't let her ruin the whole night. I just won't. I know her senior Prom wasn't all she wanted, but it's not about her anymore. It's my turn. I've got this."

Lea makes sure her face is properly masked, dry, and unemotional when she walks back in her house. In as flat a tone as she can muster, she tells Mother that Mitch said no, but doesn't expound any further. She goes to her room and sets out to making her list. She adds Brian and Mitch and marks them both out and continues down the page with everyone she can think of as a possibility.

Days pass and with each setting sun hope dwindles. Once thought to be an attainable goal, the task proves much more challenging than first believed. Lea looks down at the list before her. The list grows more and more depressing as name after name gets crossed out. She's running out of time, running out of options, running out of hope.

Twenty-two names crossed out, twenty-two attempts, twenty-two rejections, twenty-two guys cross before the three cloaks huddled together. Thistle shutters and shakes as she weeps silently. The consoling capes beside her remain mute, unable to muster honest words of comfort, unwilling to inflict further pain by instilling false hope with lies.

The hourglass sand falls, every grain burying Lea, choking her with its weight. So little time remains, barely over a week, and they all said no. Lea knows if she starts crying now she might not be able to stop. She lifts up from the exhausted list and heads to the bathroom. She splashes her face with cool water and takes a good long look at herself in the mirror.

What is it that's really putting everyone off? Why did they all say no? Could it be the neon sign powered by the shiny stone on her left hand flashing across her forehead "No Chance! Don't Bother!"? Maybe it's the chestnut, copper, and golden vipers slithering on her head. If they were truly venomous, everyone would have turned to stone by now, but perhaps she is that hideous to look upon. Lea's hazel eyes shine a bright green and begin to sting with the tears that she's not allowing to fall.

Raven can take no more. "Emerald, you had a good idea, and you made a valiant effort, but now it's time for desperation. Time to expand that list."

Lea makes a quick stop back into her room and jots down two more names on the list, Jason and Troy, and then heads out to the living room to talk to Mother. "Mom may I use the phone?"

"Sure," Mother replies. She doesn't ask why, doesn't realize that Lea is still searching, completely unaware of the numerous attempts, numerous rejections, or the overall toll it is having on her youngest child.

Lea grabs the cordless and steps into the kitchen, giving the pretense that she doesn't want to disturb Mother, but honestly is seeking privacy for her call. She dials up Allie.

"Hello."

"Is Allie there?"

"It's me. What's up? How's the date hunt going?"

"Don't ask."

"I take that as you haven't found one yet?"

"Nope. Not yet. That's why I'm calling. I was

wondering if you could do me a favor?"

Raven grumbles, "She better do this for me. She said she'd help, and she's got a date to Prom. I don't."

Allie enthusiastically agrees, "Sure. Anything. What do you need?"

Lea swallows a huge gulp of her pride and rolls her eyes. "I need you to call your friend Troy for me and see if he's willing to go with me?"

"Really?"

"Yep."

"Okay."

"Give me a call back when you have an answer."

"Alright, but I don't know how long it might take me to get in touch with him."

"I'm not waiting around for each answer. I've got a couple more people to try. It's whoever says yes first at this point."

"Good plan. I'll call you as soon as I know something."

"Thanks. Later. Bye."

"Bye."

Lea hangs up the phone. One call down, one more to go.

Emerald gasps, "Troy? That's your solution? Raven, what are you doing?"

Raven retorts, "Fixing this anyway I have to."

"But he's such a jerk!"

"Jerk, yes, but he's taller than me, blonde and kind of cute."

"Cute doesn't make up for his disgusting ego though. We're talking about a guy that suggests and goes on double dates to restaurants where he can ogle other scantily clad women in too tight t-shirts and booty shorts!"

"I don't think they can actually be declared double dates

when it's just him and two girls."

"Exactly my point!"

"Would you rather go with Ginger?"

Thistle stops her rocking and lifts her hood, "I don't want to go with her. Please, Emmy, let Rae try."

Emerald's protests are completely deflated by Thistle's plea. She strokes the satin hood peering at her. "Okay." She looks across at Raven. "Do what you need to do."

Lea dials the phone again.

"Hello?" a male voice answers.

"Is Jason available?"

"You're talkin' to him."

"It's Lea."

"Hey, what's up?"

"I know you are supposed to work, and that's why you aren't going with Lauren, but I was wondering if there is ANY way you can get out of it, swap shifts or something and go to Prom with me? I've already got the tickets."

"I really can't. There's no one to cover it. I take it you aren't having much luck since John left you high and dry."

"Nope. None at all, but still trying obviously. Can you think of anyone? What time is your shift over? Maybe you could meet up with us afterwards."

"I really wish I could think of someone… anyone, but I've got nothin'. Meeting after could be a possibility. Can I get back to you on that?"

"Sure. I'll talk to you at school. You can let me know then."

"Okay. Good luck."

"Thanks."

"Bye."

"Bye."

Lea hangs up the phone again. She sits at the table,

lightly banging her head with the phone. Who has she missed? There's got to be someone. She gets an idea and grabs the phonebook. She doesn't know the number and doesn't want to have to ask her parents. There it is. Once again she dials.

"Hello?" It's her father's best friend.

"Is Ross there?" Lea asks hoping this doesn't become a huge issue if or when it gets back to her dad.

"No. He's staying at his mother's."

"This is Lea. May I have the phone number to her house? I really need to ask him something."

"She doesn't have a phone right now. Everything okay?"

"Not really. Could I leave a message for him with you in case you see him in time?"

"Sure."

"I have Prom this coming Saturday, and John isn't able to make it back to take me. I have an extra ticket but don't have anyone to go with me. I was wondering if Ross would be willing to be my escort for the evening?"

"I'll pass it along when I see him, but I don't know when that will be for certain."

"Thank you. I appreciate it."

"You're welcome."

"Bye."

"Bye."

Lea drops her head as she hangs up the phone again with no success. She returns the phone to Mother and heads back to her room. She adds Ross' name to the list and crosses out Jason. She curls up on her bed and buries her face in Greenie, her security blanket. A thinning baby blanket that has lost all of its edging but that she has had since the day she was born, it's her most treasured possession, always there to catch her tears, never criticizing, never comparing her to her near perfect glowing sibling, never abandoning her, never expecting her to be anything other than what she is, and never disappointing her. Greenie feels soft against her skin as he once again catches her tears and muffles her sobs.

Thistle curls up in a ball on her side, Greenie wadded up as a pillow under her head, Emerald rubbing her shoulder and back, completely drained of any further ideas. Her lime hood shifts as she glances over to the dark shroud. "What now? Just wait?"

Raven looks down at Thistle and then to Emerald. "I have one last thing I can try, but I doubt it will pan out. I'll go tomorrow. It really was a good idea, Emerald, even if it doesn't work out."

Everyone fades into shadow. Rose alone steps forward. There's something more that you must know that they are all completely unaware of. Ginger, the seemingly evil sister, has been reading in her room, which she often does. She has overheard the phone calls and Lea's crying. Although she is lying across her bed feigning ignorance to her sister's plight, she's collecting information and assessing the situation. Furthermore, Ginger also reads Lea's diary when she's not around, feeling free to share these private thoughts with Vikki or whomever else she wants to, Ginger's version of payback for everything Lea writes about her, but right now, that diary contains Lea's anxiety, panic, and heartbreak as well as the list of names, almost all crossed out. Rose steps back, and everyone returns where they had been.

Lea falls asleep quickly from mental exhaustion, but it's not a restful slumber. Her mind races with images of Ginger glowing radiantly and looking beautiful. Standing next to her is a dull, lackluster silhouette in frumpy, drab rags, with hair frayed and fuzzed as a rat's nest. Ginger talks, laughs, cavorts, and whirls across the floor, instantly fitting in better than the wallflower left holding her bag had been able to muster in all her years with these people. The shrinking violet withers and wilts into a tattered lump in the corner. Lea wakes feeling unrested and mentally dejected.

Early the following afternoon Lea asks Mother if she may borrow the car to run over to the Logans' house. Mother says sure and waves her hand towards the entry table where the keys are, but not inquiring further as to why she'd be going. Lea notices that her mom looks tired today. She's drained and lies back on the couch.

Lea pauses before she leaves. "Do you need anything before I go? Something to drink? Are you hungry?" she inquires.

"No. I'm fine. Ginger's here, isn't she?" her mother leans her head back to try and look in Lea's general direction.

"I think she's reading or something in her room. Want me to get her?" Lea asked.

Raven grumbles, "I don't really feel like dealing with her right now. Just tell her to yell if she needs something."

"Raven... Come on. Look at her. Give her a break already," Emerald urged.

"I'm not in the mood right now, and it's her brainiac idea that's soured my disposition," Raven half barked back at her green counterpart.

"Because you're normally such a fresh blooming flower," even Emerald was uncharacteristically snide.

Once again Thistle's almost painful whimper alters their focus, "Rae, Emmy, please, don't. I'm so tired. I just want to sleep."

"Shhhh... little one. It's fine. We'll stop," Emerald returns

to rubbing Thistle's back and coaxing her to sleep again.
Raven returns to listening for Mother's answer.

"Just let her know you're leaving and be back before dinner," Mother slid her head back down towards the television, and Lea knew she'd probably be out soon. Mother didn't really watch tv that often. She usually just listened to it while reading or crocheting or something else, but her eyes weren't granting her the perfect vision she once had and, if she wasn't even trying, she'd be asleep quickly.

"Sure," Lea answered, heading back to inform her sister and knowing she better be back before dinner because Mother was in no condition to cook and Lea rarely enjoyed the overly creative culinary attempts that Ginger subjected them to. Besides, Ginger's only home on the occasional weekends from college. She doesn't know what Mom can and cannot tolerate. The last thing the fragile woman needs on a bad day is Ginger whipping up something that sets Mother's stomach to turn with just the smell.

Lea stops outside Ginger's door, not wanting to put too much effort into any interaction with her sister. "Hey, I'm heading out. Mom's probably gonna be out soon, but she wanted you to know I wasn't here."

"Okay," Ginger acknowledges with as little interest as possible. Lea is shocked to see that she appears to actually be getting up as she turns and heads out. Lea starts the car and looks up to see Ginger walking into the living room. Lea watches as she plops into a recliner, pulls her knees up and goes back to reading her book.

Emerald expresses the shock of all, "At least she'll hear if Mom needs something."

"Yeah, yeah, yeah... Can I go now? I'm not eating any weird crap because I don't get back in time." Raven's mood doesn't improve with the revelation.

"She still has a couple finals this week. She'll be gone tomorrow, at least for a few days. I think you can survive a few more hours, Raven."

"I know. I know. Only here to bring back some of her crap early..." Raven grumbles. *"And to rub my reality in my face,"* she mumbles to herself.

Lea backs out and heads towards the Logans' house, her stomach in knots and her mind racing. She has no idea how to pull this off, and she's pretty sure she's just wasting her time and effort, but she's also out of options. A glimpse of her having to stand next to that perfectly petite pigmy flashes in her head. The fear and anxiety infuse her with the resolve to try, to focus on the task at hand, and to pay attention to the road so she doesn't wreck the car.

"That would be just what we need right now," Raven spouts off. *"Dad comes home from work tonight to see I've crashed the car. I'd be so busted! At least I wouldn't have to worry about the whole Prom date thing because I think he'd ground me for the rest of my life."*

Lea pulls into the drive and shuts off the car. As she opens the door to get out she looks up to see Mitch walking across the lawn towards her.

"How does he do that?" Emerald's tone perks up. *"How does he know I'm here to talk to him? Freaky!"*

"Or maybe he just drew the short straw because nobody else wants to deal with me," Raven retorts.

"Just remember this is your idea, and stop being such a downer. This is hard enough already," Emerald chastises the dark figure.

Lea strolls up to Mitch, trying to be as casual as she can muster. "Hi."

"Hello," Mitch stops in front of her.

"How do you always know when I'm here to see

you?"

"Lucky guess." Mitch has his standard don't you wish you knew what I'm really thinking smirk parked firmly across his face. It's like he's always privy to some inside joke that you can only wish that you are included in on, like he always knows more than you do or more than you want him to.

"I guess there's no point beating around the bush. I'm desperate, and you are quite literally my last hope. I'm out of time. I'm out of ideas. I haven't been able to find a date, and, trust me, I have tried. Is there anything I can say to you or to your brother to get you to change your mind?"

Mitch started walking towards the two lawn chairs in the middle of the yard. They were set to make the most of the shade, but also kept a distance from the house. Lea follows and takes her seat next to him. He faces the house, allowing Lea's voice to be carried away into the trees and nothingness as they speak.

"I truly am sorry, but I can't. Have you tried...?"

Lea cuts him off. "I have tried everyone I know. They either already have a date, are working, or some other reason made up so they don't have to say they just don't want to go with me. I've even gone so far as to ask my friends to ask their friends and, although I haven't heard back on that yet, I'm not getting any warm and fuzzy feelings of hope from it. So far, including the no call backs and you, I've been turned down twenty-six times."

"Really? Twenty-six?"

"I told you. I've tried."

Mitch is speechless, which is odd. Usually he only holds his tongue to keep from saying something he probably shouldn't, but that's not the case now. His playful smirk is gone.

Lea crumbles, letting the rush of frustration pour out, "How can Mom make me take her? She hates me."

"Well it's not like you're overly fond of her."

"Because she hates me! I've done everything I know how to do to get her to like anything about me, anything I do, to get her approval in any way possible. Doesn't matter."

"It's nothing you've done."

Lea stares down at the grass. "Yes, it is. I was born. Did anyone ever tell you what the first thing she said when they brought me home from the hospital?"

"Not that I'm aware of."

"She said 'It's not a boy. Take it back.'"

"That's not why she hates you."

"Then why? What did I ever do to her that was so horrible. I idolize her. I envy her. For years I've wanted to be like her, be as smart as her, to have half of her talent, a smidgen of her beauty."

"You do."

"Please… If that were remotely true, why would she treat me like a dirt clod that she can't scrape off her shoe?"

"Because you don't have to work for any of it."

"What?" Lea's voice is laced with her confusion. She looks up at Mitch to see if this is just another joke of his twisted humor, but there's nothing but sincerity in his features, confusing her even more.

"How long do you study each night?"

"Not that much, if at all."

"And when she was in school?"

"Couple hours maybe."

"What kind of grades do you get?"

"Mostly A's, couple B's."

"And her?"

"A's and B's as far as I know"

"Who's got the higher GPA?"

"Me."

"Getting it yet?"

"But she can draw, and write, and her musical talent is well beyond mine."

"Maybe instrumental, but from what your mother says about you, not vocal. And I thought you write too."

"Just poetry. She said it sucks and won't even read it now if I ask her." Lea takes a mocking tone as she adds, "She says poetry isn't her thing."

"Did she ever like poetry?"

"I thought she did. I thought she liked Poe and Dickinson, which is why I started to read them."

"Hmm," Mitch raises his eyebrows, hoping Lea is starting to get the picture, a hint of the smirk returning.

"Are you going to deny that she's gorgeous?"

"She's pretty, but so are you."

Lea just shoots him an 'are you kidding me' look.

"How many boyfriends did she have in school?"

"None really."

"And what's this?" Mitch lifts her left hand. "Maybe you're just an ugly duckling that needs to realize she's growing up, no more fluffy feathers."

"She calls me an amazon."

"Only because she wishes she could be taller than what she is." His grin is back in full force now.

Lea starts feeling better in spite of herself. Mitch is good at making people smile, even when they don't want to. "Doesn't really change the fact that it's going to suck having to go with her."

"Quite possibly, but try to make the best of it and ignore any snide comments she throws."

"At least, you acknowledge that much. Mom just

doesn't get it."

"Why don't you tell her?"

"Same reason you don't want to ruin your brother's Prom. We weren't raised to deliberately hurt our family members if we can avoid it. She's still got good days and bad days, and the last thing she wants to hear is that her daughters don't have that super close knit Brady Bunch kind of bond with each other."

"Understood."

Lea stands from her chair. "I've gotta get going. I have to get home before Ginger starts making some horrid concoction for dinner."

Mitch walks her back to her car. "I really am sorry I can't help you out."

"You'll let me know if you think of anyone that's not busy this Saturday?" she asks before sliding behind the wheel.

"Of course," Mitch smiles and closes the door behind her.

"Thanks," she answers through the open window, starts the car, and backs up to turn around. Mitch turns and heads back across the lawn to the house as she pulls away and heads back home.

"Well, that brings me back to the crashing the car option," Raven can't help herself.

"Tell me you aren't actually pondering that." Emerald is concerned, but keeping her voice low so as not to disturb Thistle, still curled up and sleeping.

"Maybe a little bit."

"Dad will totally blow a gasket, and don't forget graduation is coming up."

"I said maybe." Raven sulks, defeated.

When Lea walks in, she lets Mother know she's back

and heads to the kitchen. Nothing's started yet.

"YES!!!" Raven and Emerald both throw their arms up in triumph. Thistle stirs, and Emerald quickly returns to soothing her so as not risk waking her. The bad news can wait.

Ginger comes in and stops before she's completely through. "Allie called while you were gone. She said to call her back."

"Thanks. I'll call her after I get dinner started." Lea didn't want to leave an opening for Ginger to cook. She starts pulling random items... meat something, nuked potatoes, and she'll whip up a quick iceberg salad after she gets off the phone.

After everything is well established, Lea grabs the phone, hoping Allie has some good news for her. She really needs some good news about now.

"Hello." It's Allie.

"Hey. I heard you called."

"Yeah, heard from Troy," Allie's tone is not encouraging.

"Please, tell me it's good news."

"Wish I could."

"Know what? I don't even want to hear the reason why. Don't tell me. I don't want to know."

"Okay. I take it you're still dateless."

"Yep."

"I'm sorry."

"Not your fault. Thanks for tryin'. I've got to finish dinner," which although true, also makes for a good excuse not to stay on the phone or on the subject any longer.

"See ya tomorrow."

"Bye."

Lea hung up the phone and turns to find Ginger passing back through. "Umm... Nobody else called while I was gone, did they?"

"No," she answers and continues on her way.

Lea sets back to dinner, trying to pretend she's not bothered by any of the events today, or in the last few months.

The eternal optimist, Emerald, tries to alter the focus. "Mitch was very nice today."

"Did you miss the point where he shot us down...? Again," Raven replies, not sure if she's trying to be annoyingly positive or just wasn't paying attention to what actually happened.

"No. I got that part, but the rest of it was quite nice of him to say."

"I think I'm going to puke."

"But you haven't eaten yet."

"The situation hasn't changed, and there's nothing further I can do. Do you have some secret plan hidden beneath those folds that you've failed to share with me?"

"No. No, I don't, but I don't see the point in making it worse for Thistle. She upsets so easily, and it's going to be hard enough as it is. So if you don't mind, try to keep that in mind between now and Saturday."

"Point well made. I'll try, but I make no promises." Raven concedes.

Before bed, Lea crosses both Troy and Mitch off her list. It made sense at the time to put Mitch's name down again since it was two distinctly different attempts. Now it just makes the list seem longer.

That night Thistle's worst nightmares consume Lea's mind. She sees Ginger standing beside her in her royal blue, one shoulder, fit and flare gown with silver accents. Even in heels, she isn't as tall as Lea, but it doesn't matter. She makes a statement as she glides into the ballroom. Lea might as well be wearing a burlap sack next to her. Heads turn and everyone points and laughs. Lea, the pathetic, has to bring her sister to Prom. The laughter echoes louder and louder. Lea tries to cover her ears, but it just makes the laughter echo louder within her head until it is no longer bearable and she wakes with a start to the sound of her alarm clock, the pounding in her head growing more apparent despite the fact that the nightmare has ended. Well, that particular version of her nightmare has ended.

　　She gets ready for school and goes through the motions of her day, not really registering the conversations or interactions she's having, preferring instead to try and remain numb, to ignore the excitement of everyone around her as they solidify their plans. She can't share their bliss, and yet she also can't completely accept her fate. She never turned in the name of her date for the place card. She held on to hope until it was too late to add any name, even Ginger's.

　　"Raven, did you do that on purpose?" Emerald can't let it go.

　　"No, but I wish I'd had the thought." Raven is amused more than offended.

　　"Do you think she'll get mad when she notices?" Thistle asks, genuinely concerned.

　　"I doubt it. Not enough to make an issue of it while we're there." Emerald tries to reassure her.

　　"Whatever." Raven smiles to herself enjoying the unintended slight. "You know, if we avoid pictures, there won't be any permanent tangible marks that she has infected the night at all."

　　"You can't be serious." Emerald gasps.

　　"I'm okay with that, Emmy." Thistle's small voice always surprises Emerald when she agrees with Raven.

　　"We'll see when the time comes." Emerald pats Thistle's

hood as she considers the idea further. She turns to Raven before continuing. "You're a bad influence on her."

"I accept that, but there's going to come a day when you're going to have to admit out loud that I'm also the best protection she's got," Raven acknowledges with an eerie confidence.

"That may be, but today is not that day." Emerald hugs Thistle close to her, unwilling to relinquish her to whatever future Raven is alluding to.

"We'll revisit this conversation on Sunday." Raven almost caws as she spins, letting her cloak swirl around in a large circle before landing again on her perch.

School now over, Lea returns home with no real clue of what has happened throughout the day. She wants to hope that Ross called back, but that's not how reality has played out this far.

The next forty-eight hours passes the same way. Her sleep is plagued with nightmares instead of rest and the world moves around her without her really being a participant in it. Ross doesn't call. Nothing changes.

Mother is sitting in the living room as Lea walks through the door Wednesday afternoon. She's on the phone and very excited. Obviously she's feeling better than she had over the weekend and having a much better day than Lea. "Good news, Lea!" Mother can hardly contain herself.

"What?" Lea struggles to keep her tone polite and respectful.

"Don't you dare make me play some stupid guessing game! I don't feel like entertaining you today." Raven's bitterness towards KewpieMom grows each day that passes, bringing the dread ever closer.

"Ginger got you a date to Prom!" Mother is overjoyed at her news, which is completely contrary to her original decree.

"WHAT!?!" *All three cloaks focused on KewpieMom in disbelief, relief, and bewilderment.*

"How did this come about? I didn't think she was even due back 'til tomorrow night," Lea is befuddled by the news and failing in her attempt not to feel ungrateful.

KewpieMom points to the phone. "She just called between classes so I could tell you," KewpieMom beams with pride for her golden child. She hands the phone to Lea.

"Who?" Lea inquires cautiously.

"Dave Johnson. He isn't doing anything this weekend. I said I'd owe him a favor." Ginger's tone dripped with how inconvenient it was to ask him and how Lea should be groveling with appreciation for having to put her out like that.

"Oh. Thanks," Lea gives the phone back to her mother and steps out of the room pretending she has some homework to attend to.

"I can just imagine what that favor might be that he's hoping for..." Raven mumbles under her breath as she imagines stripper music and a cheap hotel room.

"Doesn't matter what they may have set up in exchange. I don't have to put out for it, and Ginger won't be there. The night is saved, and all our friends will be at the same table so there's no way we can have a bad time." Emerald practically jumps up and down as she replies to Raven's slight. She hugs Thistle close to her. "It'll all be alright now. Nothing to worry about. He's got a cute little car too, so it'll be a fun drive there and back. It's all going to fine." Thistle hugs her back and Emerald gives her a kiss on the head and begins rocking back and forth still cradling the small, fragile figure in her arms.

~ *Prep And Plan* ~

Lea floats through the next three days. All is again
well and life is good despite how much she misses John. It's
still going to be a fabulous night, made special by all those
wonderful people she calls friends. Lauren will be there with
Brian. Allie is going with Carl. DiAna has warned everyone
that her date, Nick, is a couple years older than she is and is
also blind, which is a first for most of us, but okay. No
biggie. Michelle and Mike are going together, and Gail is
going with Andy Rook. We all just call him Rook. He's not
even cool enough to play a geek on a bad television sitcom,
but at least Gail has a date, and she thinks he's nice enough,
which is really all that matters.

"It does make sense," Emerald politely demands Raven's
attention, "because rooks in chess move kind of screwy and Andy
acts kind of screwy."

"You know I like you, right? Well, as much as I like
anyone...," Raven responds.

"Yeah."

"Then I hope you aren't too horribly offended when I tell

51

you that, for as intelligent as you are, sometimes you're an idiot."

Emerald's mouth drops open, "Excuse me?"

"You're thinking of the horses, right?"

"Yeah."

"Those are called knights. Rooks are the castles on the ends. Still fits as I've found them to be rather two dimensional and lacking depth."

"Oh," Emerald slumps at her faux pas.

"They do become more impressive as the game continues, assuming they make it that long, so maybe there's hope for him later in life. That might make you feel better, but I don't care either way. To be completely honest, I think Gail's really doing him a favor. By showing up with a girl, people might stop thinking he's gay," Raven relates her observation with utter nonchalance as she lounges on her bench.

"Why do you always have to be so mean?" Emerald replies as she throws a glance in Thistle's direction, perpetually wondering what negative influence Raven may be having on this young girl. Will her hard shell and cynicism eventually rub off and make this sweet, vulnerable, fragile wee one disappear altogether?

Thistle lies stretched out on her stomach coloring fanciful pictures, apparently unaware and unaffected by the conversation volleying above her.

"I don't consider it mean if I'm just expressing an honest observation. I just say what others keep to themselves," Raven continues.

"Well, you can keep that one to yourself too. True or not, it's just plain mean. What does it matter anyway if he is?"

"I couldn't care less one way or the other, but you know as well as I do living here, at this moment in time, being openly gay is not in a person's best interest."

"I'm just glad everyone else doesn't have to hear what you say like I do. Do you think you can try to behave around him?"

"There will be plenty of other people to talk to. I can ignore him easily enough. We've been in the same building for how long now? I know his name, what he looks like, and very little else beyond that because he comes across as too weird even for me, which is saying an awful lot. I like to think I embrace the oddity in people, but he's like some troll that I imagine living in his own little world under some bridge that I do my very best never to cross over."

"Any chance you would be willing to disappear for a while so I don't have to wonder if you're going to cause trouble?" Emerald jests.

"Nope," Raven's grin shines from beneath her hood, "but I promise to read a book and try to keep my mouth shut."

Emerald knows this is the best she can hope for and decides to change the subject, "What do you think Dave will wear?"

"Considering how much time he's been given, I don't think you have a right to be too terribly picky."

"You don't think he'll show up in jeans, do you?"

"If you're that worried about it, call him up and ask him?"

"I can't do that. It would seem ungrateful and rude."

"Then don't worry about it."

"Slacks. If he just has a pair of nice slacks and a black sweater, that'll work." Emerald paces as she ponders Dave's attire. Raven ignores her and contemplates the rest of the evening's plan.

Although Jason has to work, he's going to meet up with everyone afterward at the diner. Once we're all there, we'll go to the after party at Shane's house. Brian knows where it is so we'll all just follow him. All the plans are coming together nicely. Raven's attention is disrupted when the phone rings. Emerald is unphased, still pondering over Dave's wardrobe.

Lea's dreams ease to the usual ache of missing John, and sleep is once again much more restful, the black cloud of doom gone from above her. Another day at school dawns. This time she smiles as people talk about their plans and notices others as they pass her. She seeks out Mr. Peters, one of the class sponsors and organizers of the Prom.

"Mr. Peters?" Lea catches him in the hall outside his classroom.

"Yes?" He turns to see who's calling for him.

"I know I was supposed to get you the name of who is going with me Saturday a long time ago, but I honestly didn't have anyone until yesterday." Lea starts to explain.

Mr. Peters nods as she continues, "Is there any way at all to get his name added now?"

"I'm sorry, but there isn't. We are too far past the deadline." Mr. Peters shakes his head from side to side as he delivers the news.

"That's what I figured, but I thought I'd ask anyway." Lea shrugs her shoulders. "Thanks."

Mr. Peters tilts his head and grins helplessly before having his attention diverted by another student.

Lea turns and goes on her way, not even noticing the boy he is now speaking to is Rook.

"There. I tried. Dave can't hold it against us now. I put forth an honest effort as soon as I could," Emerald states, proud of herself for thinking of the idea.

The last couple days flew by quickly. Everyone made their arrangements to get down there on their own. DiAna and Nick would be riding with Rook and Gail. Mike would be driving Michelle down in his car, and Lea of course would get to go in Dave's cute, little, red sports car.

Carl and Allie would be in his parents' van, which might have been more concerning to Allie's parents if she had liked him in any way shape or form other than just as a nice guy that can get her to her best friend's Prom. For whatever reason, Allie can't see him in a romantic way, but Carl is always a respectful gentleman towards her.

"Emerald, why do you have such a soft spot for Carl?" Raven inquires.

"Because if what they say is true, that nice guys finish last, he'll be lucky to finish at all." Emerald shocks Raven with the bluntness of her response. "He is always the sweetest guy. He deserves someone who appreciates that about him. Allie may not see him that way, but at least he gets to say that he got to take a girl he really liked to his Prom. It may mean more to him than her, but I hope she understands enough by seeing what I'm going through that she tries to make it special... within reason of course."

Raven nods her understanding, "True. Very true."

Friday evening Lea makes sure to set everything out in advance. Her dress is ready and hanging on her door, heels on the floor underneath. Her purse is on the kitchen table, tickets, wallet and a small vile of perfume inside. She calls Allie to verify times and plans for the rest of the evening. Satisfied that there's nothing more she can do, she gets ready for bed. She gives her parents a hug and kiss goodnight and is about to head off to the land of nod when the phone rings.

Ginger answers. "Hello? ... Why are you asking me? ... I have no idea. ... She's right here. Ask her." She hands the phone over to Lea.

"Hello?" Lea answers.

"Hey. It's Dave." He is unexpectedly polite.

"Oh. Hey! What's up?" Lea inquires in an upbeat tone.

"If he's calling to cancel, I'm going to lose it!" Raven is suddenly alert and hypersensitive to what his next words might be. Her alarm puts her fellow cloaked figures on edge.

"I was wandering what time you want me to come by to pick you up?" Dave asks.

All three robes let out an obvious breath of relief and their shoulders fall to a relaxed position.

"Oh… Let me look." Lea grabs the tickets to see what time it starts. She returns to the phone. "Well it says it's all supposed to get started around six, and it's on the north side of Capital City, so is five too early?"

"Nah. Five is fine. I'll be there."

"ASK HIM!" Raven shouts in Lea's head.

"No. It'll be rude." Emerald tries to keep Raven from screaming.

"ASK HIM ALREADY!" Raven screams again.

"Ummm… I'm wearing a peach dress, but it has some black on it, so, if you had a black sweater, that should look okay." Lea chokes out, not trying to offend the one guy that's saving her.

"Oh, I got a tux." Dave pops back.

"Really?" Lea chuckles a little. "Awesome. I didn't think you'd have enough time for that. Cool." Lea's surprise and relief came through as a smile in her tone.

"See, Raven. Things are turning around." Emerald beams with happiness. She grabs Thistle and starts spinning the little girl around in circles as they skip and dance.

"Touché. So they are…" Raven concedes to her point with a deep sigh and watches the pair as they dance, tapping her foot, but not joining in the ecstatic silliness that the pair exudes.

"Well, I didn't, but Chris has one and he's letting me borrow it." Dave says.

"Is there anything else?" Lea asks.

"Nope. That's about it. Can I talk to Ginger again?" Dave inquires.

"Sure. Here she is." Lea passes the phone back to her

sister.

Lea pretends she can't hear the conversation that follows, but Raven takes note of what's heard and lets her imagination fill in the blanks… in the worst possible way.

"What's up?" Ginger asks, the tone of her voice much nicer for others than it is for Lea. "Yeah. I heard about it."

"Heard about what?" Raven wonders.

"I was thinking about it, so probably, yeah,." Ginger answers.

"I bet she was thinking about it…" Raven sneers.

"Sure. I'll already be there before you two get back, but I'll see you when you get there. Later." Ginger hangs up the phone.

"So he's looking to get paid out that same night. Good to know." Raven takes note of the expected schedule for that evening. "Well, if he's going to be in a rush to get to Ginger, I should ask KewpieMom if I can borrow the car when we get home so I can go out with everyone else. This actually might be even better. He won't have to pretend he really wants to be around my friends, and I won't have to act like I don't know his kindness isn't because he's hoping to get laid by my sister."

Emerald almost sings her response and doesn't quit dancing, "It's not likely that Ginger will actually sleep with him. You know that, right?"

"I'm very well aware of that. I also don't give a rat's butt if she does or doesn't as long as she doesn't screw up my having a date tomorrow." Raven's snarky tone floats freely now and with such ease with things finally falling into place. "I just don't want him figuring that out between now and then and NOT taking me because he's not going to get the payout he's hoping for."

"Fair enough," Emerald's focus is caught by the phone ringing again. "Wow. Isn't this a popular house tonight?"

"Hello?" Ginger answers. "Hang on. She's right

here." She hands the phone out. "It's for you. It's your lover boy," her tone dripping with sarcasm and condescension.

"Hello?" Lea addresses the caller.

"Hi, Honey." John's voice is so soothing to her.

"Hi." Lea's tone changes to a soft lilt in recognition. She walks back to her parents' room and flops down on their bed.

"How are you doing?" John asks.

"I miss you."

"Miss you too."

"Wish you were going with me tomorrow."

"I know, Honey. I wish I was too."

"So why aren't you on a damn plane?" Raven's hostility bursts forth.

"Because he's trying to make a better life for you," Emerald defends him.

"And he couldn't wait a couple more months to set out on this plan? Maybe after I graduated? Would it have killed him?" Raven demands. "I was there for everything for his senior year."

"I don't know. I'm sure he just didn't think about it like that." Emerald's shield is weakening.

"So is your Mom really making you take Ginger?" John continues completely unaware of what Lea is really thinking.

"No. She found me a date a couple days ago." Lea answers him.

"Your mom or your sister?"

"My sister."

"Oh! That's good. Who?"

"Dave Johnson."

"At Least you're not stuck with her."

"I guess," Lea grumbles.

"But he's not you!" Emerald cries out as if she expects him

to hear, momentarily leaning towards Raven's point of view.

"And there's that undisclosed favor he's going to want to cash in...." Raven adds.

"It'll be fine. I'm sure you're gonna have fun. Allie's still gonna be there, right? Nothing changed there?" John tries to be positive.

"Yea, she's still going. Wait. You used her name. You never call her by her name. I wasn't sure you even knew her name."

"Of course I know her name."

"Then why do you always call her 'what's her name'?"

"Because it bugs her," John's voice smiles.

Lea chuckles.

Raven interjects, "This is why he gets away with crap. He's convinced everyone thinks that he's a good guy all the time so nobody ever suspects that his stunts might be deliberate and calculated."

"I don't think he's as devious as you're implying," Emerald contradicts.

"Really?" Raven plots. "You don't think so?"

"What?" Emerald knows not to trust the intonations in Raven's voice

"Wait for it..." Raven instructs.

Lea's hesitant, "Umm... I've been wondering about something."

"Shoot," John invites her to elaborate.

"Before you left, we had pizza over here with my family one night..."

"We've done that a couple times. Can you narrow it down?"

"Ginger was being mouthy and picking on us, slash me, more than usual..."

"She always does that. Can you be more specific?"

"We were on the couch, and she was sitting on the floor by the tv."

"Ahh. That time."

"Yeah. That time."

"What about it?"

"You walked over, stood towering over her, and poured soda in her face."

"Yeah? So?"

"So she was ready to pound you, and my mother jumped to your defense saying there's no way you did it deliberately. You must not have known how full the can was, yadda, yadda, yadda..."

"Yeah. I remember that. What's your point?"

"My point is I'd barely taken a sip or two out of that can. You had to have known it was all but full."

"I knew."

"You did that on purpose, didn't you?"

"Of course I did. I knew exactly how full it was."

"Why'd you let my mother defend you like that? She truly believes it was an accident."

"Well, nobody was telling Ginger to knock it off, and I'd had enough."

"I TOLD YOU!" Raven points emphatically at Emerald, vindicated. "I KNEW IT!" Emerald stands silent, stunned at the admission.

"Unbelievable. You know you have my mother completely fooled. She thinks you're this infallibly nice guy." Lea rolls over on the bed.

"I know," she can hear the smirk on his face. "Why would I want to ruin that by letting her know anything else? Why would you?"

"No reason I guess, except there are times I think my

family likes you better than they do me."

"I know, but I still like you."

"Only like? I thought you loved me. That didn't take long," Lea teases.

"Stop it. You know I love you."

"Just checking."

"I hate to do this, but I've got to get some sleep. There's an early study session in the morning."

"I was heading to bed anyway."

"Love you."

"I love you, too. Sweet dreams." Lea blows him a kiss through the phone and hangs up.

That night finds Lea relaxed and back to her hopeful dreaming, taking her to the best possibilities of the coming evening. She's getting prepped and curled and polished by her sisters in the back of the house and hears the door open. Her parents are talking to the young man that's entered their home. Although she can't make out their words, the voices are full of anticipation and smiles. She dons her dress and heels and heads to the front of the house.

She's looking down making sure she doesn't trip over the only step in the entire house, which she's done more times than she can count. Her eyes lift to see a small but delicate peach wrist corsage in his hand. She lifts her head further to realize that although he's in black, it's not a tux, nor is this Dave. It's John! He's here, in front of her in his working uniform, looking just as sharp as he did a few weeks ago only this time he includes the black tie. Lea is frozen for a moment, then lunges at him, wrapping her arms around him and giving him a big kiss with no concern to whether or not her parents would approve.

"What? How? I don't care. You're here." Lea sputters out.

"Lea, you need the tickets," KewpieMom hands Lea her purse, which has been pre-packed with tickets, cash and touch ups for her make up. "Can I get a picture before you go?"

Lea nods, but has given up the ability to speak, letting the smile that's plastered on her face speak for her. Ginger steps up and grabs her face. "Have to fix this first," she states while replacing the lipstick that's now smeared all over John, "and you might want to wipe it off." She hands him a handkerchief. "Did anyone let Dave know about this yet?"

"No," KewpieMom answers, "but you won't mind calling him, would you, Ginger? Let these two go ahead and go. Make sure to tell him thank you anyway."

"Fine," Ginger huffs just a little and heads for the phone. Lea can't hear a single word of the conversation despite the fact that she's only three feet away.

The camera flashes picture after picture and Lea and John head out to his father's luxury sedan. He opens the door for her and closes it gently after she pulls her skirt in completely. As soon as he pulls out of her driveway, he takes her left hand in his, glances down at the solitaire he gave her, and then pulls it up to his lips, kissing the back of her hand and causing her to flush.

John drives with one hand, not willing to relinquish Lea's back to her for the remainder of their trip. Still overexcited and in shock, she tries to spark a conversation, "Did you bring clothes to change into? I was supposed to be going to an after party." Lea tries to share the original plan. "Why didn't you tell me you were coming home?"

"I didn't know I was. It was a last minute thing. You don't mind, do you?" John asks with a mischievous smirk on his face.

"Not at all," Lea sighs, completely twitterpated with the man sitting next to her. He leans over and kisses her lightly, trying not to mess up the look Ginger feverishly painted back on her after their initial kiss. Lea puddles into mush.

"No, I didn't grab anything, but we'll figure that out later. You didn't grab anything either," John points out smiling at her.

"I have my clothes laid out at the house. I was planning on being dropped off there before the second half of the night. I was so shocked when I saw you and I didn't think to grab them."

"Maybe we won't need any at all..." John winks.

Lea blushes but doesn't shoot him down. She hadn't considered that at all lately because he wasn't supposed to be here. They hadn't crossed that line as of yet, but now that possibility would prance through her head all night, and she was really glad she took the extra time to shave.

They get their pictures taken, have a good dinner, talk, and laugh. She knows he doesn't like to dance and doesn't want to leave his side, so she just scoots her chair closer to his and holds his hand under the table. She has no idea who gets crowned Prom court and honestly couldn't care less. The music slows, and John stands. Lea releases her grip on his hand thinking it's just a bathroom break, but he squeezes and helps her to her feet. He leads her to the dance floor.

"I know how much you like to dance. You should get at least one song tonight." With that, he kisses her nose. Lea snuggles into him. Heart croons in the background, and they sway with the beat completely unaware of anyone or anything around them.

A voice breaks through the music. It is a misplaced

sound. It shouldn't be here, and it needs to go away. No! Don't do this! Go away! Don't make me wake up yet!

Despite the fact that she would really prefer to sleep longer and enjoy the fantasy of her dream, she learned long ago not to ignore Ginger when she says get up. If she does, her sister will come back with a glass of very cold water and dump it on her head. Lea hates it when she does that and since she has already been given instruction by both Ginger and Vikki that she is not to even attempt to get herself ready today, getting either of her sisters upset with her could have very unpleasant ramifications.

"I can just see the pictures now... lopsided, frumpy hair, face either washed out or with tacky, white-trash make-up, complete with hooker red lipstick," Raven's imaginings are enough to wake Lea quickly and with little fuss.

"Mom says you have to get your stuff done before you go, and it's going to take some time to make you look even remotely presentable." Ginger has always given such wonderfully uplifting pep talks.

"I'm up!" Lea sits up and stretches, but Ginger stands watching until she actually starts moving, knowing all too well that Lea might just lie back down again. "What's on Mom's list for today? Did she say?"

"You have to get the laundry folded and put away and empty the dishwasher." It's uncanny how much Ginger sounds like one of the evil step-sisters talking to Cinderella.

"'k. I'll be right out." Lea didn't want to give her a chance to add to the list. Ginger walks away.

"A few more zzz's would be really nice," Emerald yawns. "That was such a pleasant dream." Lea looks back down at her pillow.

With three little words, Raven chases the thought away, "Ice. Cold. Water."

Lea turns away from her bed, leaves her room and heads to the bathroom. She splashes some cool water on her face to help wake her up. Her stomach growls.

Lea slowly works her way to the kitchen with a stride that is half awake stumbling and half sleep walking. She pours a bowl of flaky sugared cereal, tops it with milk, and meanders into the living room where she plops on the couch next to Mother who is trying to match and fold a basket of socks. Between bites she turns to Mother, "I can do that. I'll get on it as soon as I finish breakfast."

"It's fine. I would appreciate you getting the clothes out of the dryer though." Mom continues her search for an ankle high white sock with a pink heel and toe without much success. She finally gives up and grabs a different sock and searches again.

Lea doesn't have the heart to tell her she just picked up the mate, so she nods her acknowledgement and continues shoveling cereal in her mouth, trying to finish the bowl before it gets too soggy. She looks around. Something's not right with this picture; the regularly occupied recliner is empty. "Where's Dad?"

"He went to play some golf. He'll be back before you leave." Mother doesn't even look up from her search.

A quick stop off at the kitchen sink and off Lea goes to complete her list. Laundry rotated – check, empty dishwasher – check, fold clothes – check, put away – check, rotate another load of laundry – check, fold – check, put away – partly.

She didn't notice what, if anything, her sisters had been doing, but the dirty dishes had magically floated and loaded themselves into the dishwasher. On Lea's way back for another arm load of clothes Ginger grabs her and pushes her into the bathroom. "You need to get in the shower now if you want to be ready in time," Ginger orders.

"But I'm not done putting the clothes away yet," Lea protests.

"*Stop pushing me around! You pixie from hell!!!*" Raven *bellows.*

"We've got it. Just get in the shower. Wash your rat's nest of hair, and don't do anything to yourself!" With that, Ginger leaves the bathroom and shuts the door behind her.

"*One of these days…*" *Raven begins and continues on mumbling under her breath with crossed arms and a scowl that can be felt beneath the shadow of her hood.*

"*She's trying to help me," Emerald cautiously counters. "And you have to admit that she does know how to get dolled up and look good.*"

"*But she doesn't have to be so rude about it.*"

"*And what would you think if she was nice and polite to me? That I had some terminal illness?*"

"*That wouldn't make a difference…. Maybe if she had a brain tumor.*" *Raven chuckles to herself.*

A small smirk curls the corners of Lea's mouth as she starts up her shower. She undresses and steps under the water. She closes her eyes and lets the hot water pound down over head. She washes from head to toe, takes extra care in shaving all the parts her dress will leave exposed just in case her dream from last night was just a foreshadowing of a very happy surprise to come, and then stands under the water again, tuning out the world, and knowing she'll probably run out of hot water soon anyway. Raven and Emerald put their arms out, swaying and twirling under a soft waterfall of liquid heat.

Suddenly, Lea's eyes fly open as the relaxing warmth is replaced by what feels like a water balloon filled with barely unfrozen liquid stolen from the underside of an iceberg hitting her back.

"Aaagh!" Lea yelps as she turns to see Ginger, empty glass in hand.

"Hurry up. We don't have forever, and you've completely steamed up the whole room," Ginger snaps quickly and pulls the curtain closed again.

"I'm gonna punch her in the face! Just let me punch her in the face!" Raven screams as Emerald grabs her arms and holds her back.

Lea turns her back to the cascade of fevered water to wash away the chill. She keeps her eyes open in case her combative sister returns with another icy water grenade. The water seems to sooth Raven's temper enough that Emerald lets her go without risking flailing arms or fists. Once Lea washes away the goose bumps, she turns off the water, steps out, and grabs a towel to dry herself off, noticing that Ginger left the door half open to try and air out the accumulated steam.

Lea is clad in undergarments and wrapped in a towel, Her sisters go to work trying to transform her into something presentable in public. Vikki tosses and tussles Lea's hair in a towel trying to wring the moisture out of it before slopping foamy goo in her hands and massaging it all over from root to tip. Ginger hands Vikki a hairdryer. She blows hot air back and forth by quickly twisting her wrist, while pulling and lifting Lea's viperous locks this way and that with her other hand.

"Emerald, can you tell me what good is it to have a head covered with snakes if they never bite anyone?" Raven inquires slightly annoyed by the yanking of hair.

"It's just your imagination. How many times do I have to tell you that? You don't have vipers slithering over your skull." Emerald leans back, doing her best to enjoy the pampering.

"Besides, think of it this way… I don't have to try and figure out what to do with my hair if I just play along and let them have their way."

"Good point, except for when the pigmy demon decided I needed shorter hair and she convinced Vikki to all but shave the back and sides of my head. Or when they tried to bleach my hair blonde and it turned out orange. It's not like it's always turns out on the good side for me." Raven's warped gratification resounds in her tone.

"Before you go off listing any more of the less than ideal outcomes, keep in mind they are the ones that primped and preened over me for last year's Prom and I think I turned out lovely." Emerald sticks her tongue out at Raven's back then returns to her spa position and puts cucumber rings on her eyes.

Vikki pulls up the reptile lair, pinning it to stay on the top of her head, occasionally using a railroad spike or two to plunge into her skull to keep it all in place. She then sets to the task of spinning the domesticated serpents into tendrils that fall and twist and stay at Vikki's command, with the help of a toxic cloud of poisonous vapor. Ginger has laid out compacts, tubes, powders, and pencils.

"I like this part. She's got her brushes and palette." Emerald's giddy with anticipation of what her artistic sister may create upon the canvas in front of her.

"Whoopee!" The sarcasm is once again dripping fluidly from Raven. "I'll end up walking out of here looking like a Picasso or a Dali."

Emerald waves her hand in the air summoning a well-built cabana boy partially clad in a white toga. He brings her a silver tray laden with grapes, sets it on a small table next to her and feeds her one before she dismisses him. She reaches for another grape and throws it full force at the back of Raven's head.

"What the…?" Raven utters.

"You said you were going to keep your mouth shut and read a book. This might be a good time for you to immerse yourself in that endeavor." Emerald pops another grape in her mouth as Raven huffs and puffs but takes the hint. A bookcase illuminates in the far corner in the back of Raven's alcove, and she floats over to it, running her finger across the spines of the dusty, ancient-looking, hardbacks. She settles on one and pulls it out, blows off some of the dust and slides it into the folds of her robe. The bookcase dims back into darkness as she floats back to her perch and settles comfortably upon her seat, trying to ignore the further primping, prodding, and preening.

"What did you decide on? 'How to Win Friends and Influence People'?" Emerald's lilt almost sings across the space.

"I'm surprised you even noticed I grabbed something with those vegetables covering your eyes? You know they're supposed to be on a relish tray and not your face, right?"

"Ha. Ha. Ha. I have to look my best and these are supposed to help with the dark circles from too many nights of crappy sleep."

"Hey, Genius... You are aware that nobody can actually see you? That only works if Lea is the frou-frou girl covering her face with healthy snack food, and I'm not gonna let that happen."

Emerald sticks her tongue out and blows a raspberry at her, otherwise completely ignoring comment. "You still didn't answer. What did you decide upon?"

"'Finding Inner Balance Beyond Ego-Id-Superego Wars'"

"Nice." Emerald turns her attention back to Ginger's mask building.

Lea closes her eyes and lifts her face towards Ginger. Fingertips and brushes ruffle through powders and dance across Lea's face. In these few stolen moments, Lea actually allows herself to believe that Ginger has some sisterly affection towards her, cares that she looks good for important events, doesn't really despise that fact that Lea is still breathing on the same planet.

Ginger snaps out soft commands now and then, "Open your eyes... Close them again... Look up... Down a little... Rub your lips together." Then she steps back and looks to see if there's anything further she can do.

"I think they're almost done." Emerald whispers with giddy excitement.

"What makes you say that?" Raven growls back.

"The look on Ginger's face and the fact that she's fussing less and less on me."

"Oh, yes the look of utter exasperation as she gives up on trying to make me look like a presentable human being..."

Ginger pulls on a curled tendril here and there trying to place them perfectly.

"Yeah. Right. Like the unruly vipers will cooperate for the rest of the night." Raven mocks Ginger's attempts.

"Whatever."

"Mirror, mirror on the wall, let me look like a pretty, pretty doll." Thistle chimes in, raising her head from her coloring.

"Great... Outnumbered," Raven concedes.

"Okay. You're done. Get dressed and try not to mess yourself up," and with that Ginger walks out.

Lea dresses and puts on her heels and notices the lack of murmurs coming from the living room, further dashing her secret hope of her dream coming true. She lays out her clothes for later before walking out for parental inspection.

KewpieMom says she looks lovely and her father gives her a positive nod. She sits gently, trying not to wrinkle the material too much while waiting for her escort.

The cloaks shift uncomfortably. A clock ticks invisibly. The metronome beat sounding more like an ancient torture than a comforting rhythm. Rocks shift in the driveway.

Lea turns and looks out the large picture window. Dave is stepping out of his car. The last spider thin strand of hope that John would be swooping in is sliced to shreds.

"Paste a smile on. It's not his fault that John's not here. It won't be polite to seem ungrateful or visibly show disappointment." Emerald reminds every one of the proper etiquette that should be followed.

Lea responds to the mental reminder in a well-rehearsed fashion, hiding her true feelings, like she's done so many times before. She smiles and greets him at the door. Dave has no flowers to gift to her.

"No flowers?" Thistle inquires to no one in particular.

"Flowers are overrated anyway. Besides, they'd just wilt and be half dead before we get back," Emerald consoles gently. Raven rolls her neck but keeps quiet. There's no point in upsetting Thistle further with her thoughts on the matter.

Raven observes Dave as he eyes Ginger, smiling at her, and, in Raven's opinion, feasts on her like a dessert buffet. Ginger smiles back. Raven lets out a low, breathy growl.

"It's not going to happen. I thought you didn't care what he fantasized about." Emerald quietly comments.

"So why is she encouraging it by smiling at him?" Raven keeps the conversation hushed so Thistle won't hear.

"I'm sure she doesn't mean anything by it. She's probably hasn't even considered that it could have crossed his mind." Emerald defends.

"But what if she has? What if she knows exactly what he's thinking and doesn't have an issue with it?" Raven contemplates the less favorable possibility.

"Enough, Raven." Emerald seethes. "Number one, you shouldn't think like that about your sister, and, number two, even thinking that it could be a reality makes me sick."

"Okay, okay. You win. It's all in his imagination and nothing's going to come of it," Raven recants.

KewpieMom pulls out her camera and snaps off a couple pictures as Lea grabs her purse, her thin wrap, and off to the car they go.

Standing next to this incredibly short sports car, Raven can no longer bite her tongue without risking drawing blood, "Why was I so hyped about this car? The seat isn't even as high as my knee. Doing squats in heels isn't exactly lady-like."

"I'll hold on to whatever I can." Emerald looks over the seat and door to find a safe spot to assure her balance.

"Just don't fall and don't crawl out on my knees," Raven tosses her advice as if it would be welcomed. "That's all I ask."

Lea eases herself into the car, her skirt falling out the door and actually dusting across the ground.

"You might want to brush that off too." Raven adds as Lea scoops up the skirt and folds it over into her lap.

"Thanks. I've got it." Emerald glares at Raven. She's had enough of Raven's helpful comments already. "Do you need a reading lamp?" Emerald points above Raven and a glaring light showers down upon the book in Raven's hands.

"Not quite that much, thank you." Raven gestures towards the light and seems to pull its energy, diming it to a warm glow. She adjusts herself for comfort and feels the bonds of her promise to stay out of things lock her in place for the remainder of the night.

~ Table Manners ~

As they set off for the venue, Lea asks, "Do you know where we're headed?"

"Yeah. It's right off the highway on the north end of town, right?" Dave replies.

"Yeah," with that confirmation the conversation concludes for the remainder of the trip. At least he has on a descent radio station. Lea watches as the car whirs past fields covered with shoots of green barely above the ground, then a quick road that juts off in a right angle to the highway, more fields, more side roads, and visibility for miles showing more of the same.

Dave looks intently into the rear view. Lea glances into the side mirror, noticing the bright red and blue flashes twirling behind them.

Raven cackles her mockery. Emerald glares at her. "What?" Raven lifts her book attempting to conceal the source of her laughter.

"It's not funny. How fast is he going anyway?" Emerald scowls with concern.

Dave pulls over into the right lane of traffic and begins to slow down. The officer flies by, lights still flashing. Dave speeds back up, but says nothing.

Emerald expels a deep sigh of relief, while Raven continues to chuckle to herself.

The view changes to buildings and more metropolitan features as they approach their destination. Dave pulls up around the back and parks the car. Lea gathers her things while he opens her door.

With a deep breath and a silent prayer that she can pull this off without falling on her face, Lea steps out and hoists herself up to her feet, thankful that she has chosen sensible heels instead of something higher.

Inside, they pass the picture station on the way to the room, which is just starting to fill. The decorations are classic, using a less is more theme. Each table centered by a small bouquet of light pink carnations, surrounded by iridescent ribbons and greenery. A curved picture frame favor stands at each setting.

Lea turns to Dave, "Shall we do pictures now, before there's a long line?"

"Sure." He answers, with no real preference what they do or when.

Lea fills out the package form and pays for the photos as another couple gets their pictures taken. Lea and Dave step in front of the skyline backdrop and smile. The flash pops and they are dismissed to go find Lea's friends and the table of fun.

Lea scans the room looking for her band of friends that will make this night a memory she'll never forget. She spots them on the far side of the room in the last line of set tables. Allie sees her at the same time, waves at her, and pops up to meet them half way.

"Hey, we're coming over to you. You didn't have to get up," Lea hugs Allie.

"I know, but I need to warn you about something." Allie's face drops as she speaks.

"What? You okay?" Lea has no idea what can have her friend so concerned.

"You aren't sitting at the same table." Allie tries to break the news as gently as she can.

"What do you mean I'm not sitting at the same table?" Lea glances up at the other people at table, most of whom are watching her reaction. "You turned in the list of who all we wanted sitting together to Mr. Peters. What happened?"

Dave hears the entire conversation unfolding around him, but he stays quiet, saying nothing.

"I have no idea. Nobody knows. We were all surprised that you weren't seated with us." Allie continues.

"Do you know where we're seated?"

"No, but I'll help you find out."

"Let me say hi first." The three of them move to the table. The girls stand, and Lea goes around giving each one a hug and says hello. The tables only seat eight, which explains why there wasn't enough room for all five couples, but it still didn't make sense that Lea should be the one to be moved when they all wanted to sit with her.

Emerald shoots Raven a disconcerting look, but, although this new development has pulled Raven's attention from her reading, she keeps her promise of silence. Thistle looks up at Emerald, "This isn't right, Emmy. This was the one thing that was supposed to be right. The one thing I could count on."

"It'll be fine, Luv." Emerald's voice is soothing and calm. "I'm sure we're at one of these other tables right around here. We'll still be close. It's not a big deal. Maybe we're sitting with Brian

and Lauren." Emerald flashes a reassuring smile, but Raven sees through its tissue paper thin veil. She knows Emerald's confidence in her words is as solid as smoke.

"It'll be easier to find our seats if we go look now. More than half the tables are still empty, so we won't have to look over and around people." Emerald voices her opinion to Thistle, hoping Lea heeds its urgency.

Greetings given, Lea catches Allie's eye and nods her head towards the rest of the ballroom. Allie excuses herself from Carl and the group and the search commences. Dave follows Lea from table to table as she circles and reads the names, not finding her own and getting further away from her band of buds.

Allie rushes up to her. Taking her by the wrist, she begins leading her between the tables, "I found your table."

"Where?" Lea wonders.

"Don't ask. It's this way." Allie threads through chairs, towards the dance floor, crosses the inlaid wood boards clicking under their feet, and slows to a stop at the second row of tables, placing them almost completely on the other side of the room.

"Thanks," Lea gives her a quick hug, honestly appreciative of her friend's help. Allie flits off back towards her own table and her own date.

Lea circles the empty table, noting the names, before taking her seat. Lea and Dave are seated with their backs against the wall, looking out at the rest of the room.

"I'm sorry you don't have your name on your place card," Lea tries to open some conversation, suddenly feeling very much in Siberia. "I told them, but it was too late."

"It's fine. I don't mind."

Emerald and Thistle are absorbing who else is to be sitting at the table, each name making Thistle more and more anxious and unsettled...

Rose lists off the roll call... Next to Dave is Krissy. She has naturally curly, crazy hair that bounces playfully and perfectly around her face. She's eternally happy, bubbly and smiles excessively. Lea knows more of her family than Krissy herself. Krissy's brother had been on the swim team with Lea years ago and her older sister had talked to Lea's mom about her cancer surgery last spring and had helped her through some difficult choices. It was years before Lea realized that the woman she knew at church as one of the most gorgeous woman she'd ever seen up close is, in fact, Krissy's aunt. The attractiveness of her gene pool had not missed Krissy.

Although Krissy's date didn't go to the same school, Lea knows who he is. Pete graduated a couple years ago, but had been a swimmer at another local school, over six feet tall, blonde, blue eyes, broad shoulders, human V with abs you can do laundry on. Lea had heard that he got a college scholarship for swimming, so most likely has not changed in build all that much. The closest Lea has ever been to him was seeing him across a pool during warm ups in years past, thankful the drool would wash away as she swam.

Tana's on Pete's right. She is one of, if not THE most popular girl in school. Captain of the rifle squad, she's intelligent, talented, and exotically beautiful, a trifecta of all that most people hope to be. She reminds Lea of Ginger without the underlying aggressive cruelty. Tana has a grace and class about her that levitates her slightly out of reach of most, coming across as aloof, mysterious and in a league well above any of the boys at their school. Lea has no idea who her date is, never even having heard his name before, but this doesn't really surprise her.

The other captain of the rifle squad, Jen, is the last girl

at the table. Although she lacks the exotic flair of Tana, she is the poster girl for American beauty. With huge blue-green hazel eyes, prominent cheek bones, button nose, full lips, beaming smile, and a flawless, sun-kissed complexion, she's a young man's erotic fantasy creation come to life.

As far as Lea is aware, Jen's been dating Eric, a percussionist that graduated last year with John who seemed to enjoy harassing Lea in the middle of the only class they had together outside of the band room. He would frequently throw comments, questions, and innuendos at her about what she and John had or had not done. Lea did her best to ignore him.

Eric and Jen are the perfectly matched couple, hammering home the rules of acceptability in percussion dating, furthering Lea's reality of how far she is from that click, how much of an outsider she is to this world, how her planet of acceptance is on the other side of the universe that is this ballroom. Ironically, Jen isn't with Eric tonight. Sitting between them instead is Ben.

Ben, admittedly less cool than the others, comes across as still awkward and trying to fit into a group that he's skirting more along the edges of but is allowed into by organizational proxy. He's percussion, so he gets to be included in the circle. He lives down the street from Lea, and they rode the same bus, but that was the extent of their interactions with each other. Lea sifts her memory for one conversation she's ever had with any of these people, but her mind remains blank.

If that was the extent of their associations, Lea could have let it go. She could have sat through one dinner, one evening, hiding within herself behind the dark safety that Raven could afford her. She could pretend that it wouldn't matter if they ignored her all night, but there is something else that all these people have in common and is assigned a seat at the next table over.

Brent and Brandi are undoubtedly one of the couples in the running for cutest couple in the yearbook. Brent is quiet, but cute and adorable in a boyish way, the guy that won't even begin to show his age until he's in his fifties easily. He smiles a great deal, but that's part of what makes him such a perfect match for Brandi, whose smile lights up every space she's ever occupied. She's bubbly and laughs a lot, although Lea has never been privy to the jokes or comments making her giggle. She, too, is unfairly beautiful, with sparkly eyes, thick bouncy hair and curves that no straight teenage boy could ignore, and she, too, is on the rifle squad.

From her seat, Lea scans the name next to Brandi's. The panic rises and begins to choke both Emerald and Thistle as the delicate child points at the table next to them. "Emmy! Do you see what I see?"

"Yes, Luv. I see it." Emerald's voice cracks.

Raven drops her book, but doesn't move from her lounged position on her perch. She's supposed to be staying out of this evening, but what is it that's freaking her cohorts out so much? Then it becomes clear as crystal. The fairies of fate and kismet are cruel and having way too much fun with Lea.

Time seems to freeze in that moment. Nobody moves. Nobody speaks. A garden of marblesque statues, all staring at one name placard facing them, at the very next table, and thankfully not yet arrived… Jackson Daniels.

Jackson is a nice enough guy, tall, handsome in his own way, and John considered him a close friend when he was still matriculating. Lea had even had a crush on him before John came along. He's polite to her on the rare occasions that they get to speak and even showed earnest concern when Lea and John had gotten in the car accident last year.

They are in last period together and both sit in the back of the room. They make up half of the cube that spins their desks and starts playing euchre the moment they get their work done. All of them are relatively intelligent, finishing rapidly and leaving loads of time for cards. This is the only time Lea and Jackson get to talk anymore since he started dating Amanda Carter this year. If he is sitting at the very next table, then there is no doubt that the placard next to his is hers. Amanda is a different story all together.

Rose is the only one moving, the only one able to speak. Lea's history with Amanda goes back years. Back in the ancient days of elementary school, they got along. Lea considered them friends, and there was no animosity between them at all.

It's ironic to recall now, but Lea can still remember when their teacher seated them all in small groups, each a different Native American tribe, and each group had to choose a chief. Of course every student voted for themselves, which made deciding a drawn out process, their first exposure to the jury system of voting again and again until a decision can be reached, albeit a unanimous verdict was not required. Lea was made chief of their tribe because while four of the five voted for themselves, Amanda cast her vote for Lea. What a different world that was and how very far from that joint cooperation they were now.

As it did with most of the people Lea had once called friends, junior high and high school changed things. Lea went her own way, and that didn't seem to be in any direction that the people her own age seemed to be going, nor did they understand or want to understand. She didn't follow their paths of popularity or parties or dating or any of that. Unlike the majority of them, Lea did not suffer from the delusion of immortality of youth. She was all too aware of the unfairness and unpredictability of death, and it had tainted her in ways nobody could comprehend.

The past year had altered Lea's perceptions of importance on everything even further. Being submissive and obedient wasn't going to cut it anymore when events grated on her like sandpaper. After Lea's Mom got sick, Lea started speaking up more. She's been on her own a lot, and if she doesn't stand up for herself, there isn't anyone else who will. Her mom has been too weak and doesn't need to be bothered with petty things that Lea can take care of for herself.

For instance, Lea found her own way of dealing with her teacher that after three quarters of the school year had passed was still calling her Ginger. So, Lea ignored her and refused to answer her, or even acknowledge that she was being spoken to, until the teacher used the proper name to address her.

As far as Amanda goes, Lea's shift in attitude had taken a more direct and confrontational path. She openly voiced her disapproval of Amanda's disrespectful tone and attitude towards KewpieMom, when her mother was trying to help out and had no business doing any of it while still fighting the issues of her treatments. Amanda insulted a costume Lea's Mother had made for her, which happened to have been KewpieMom's altered wedding dress from when she married Lea's father.

Amanda further disrespected the brand new teacher in charge, taking advantage of his inexperience and desire not to have to deal with insane high school drama from day one. Lea had started a petition to have Amanda removed from a prominent office in that class due to Amanda's unethical and disrespectful behavior. Although the petition failed, the battle lines had been drawn and classmates had either taken sides or done their best to stay completely out of the way.

Their situation was further complicated when Amanda joined the band's rifle squad her senior year, invading territory previously held sacred by Lea as a refuge, and positioning Amanda in that acceptable dating list for percussion that Lea would never attain. There was nothing left of the early friendship, no hint of those little girls, only animosity and tension.

Lea knows she is lucky to have John. Everyone else is just a friendly acquaintance, but this seating arrangement, surrounded by Amanda and Jackson's friends, people that in general don't even acknowledge Lea's existence at this school, this is unfathomable.

It's the witch's stew pot in the Hansel and Gretel stories. Lea has jumped from the frying pan, in having to bring Ginger, straight into the fire, at this table. Only this blaze is being fed directly by Dante. The searing flames grab and yank at Thistle, pulling and tugging at her, surrounding her with a suffocating smoke that swirls around her. Emerald fights to free her, but is losing control of the panic and terror that are creeping through Lea. Raven is still bound to her chair by the invisible bonds of her promise to stay out of things. Her nerves are sharpened, and she is ready to swoop in just as soon as Emerald frees her.

Dave finally notices that all the color has left Lea's face. "What's the matter?"

"All of these people hate me. I don't get along with any of them, and my nemesis is supposed to be sitting right over there." Tears well up in Lea's eyes. "I'm in hell."

"It's still better than my senior Prom," Dave tries to

ease her panic. "My date dumped me and went off and slept with someone else."

Lea rolls her eyes and can no longer keep the tears from falling. She tries to smile at him in gratitude for his less than successful attempt to cheer her up, but all she can muster is a half smirk. "Excuse me." Lea gets up and rushes off to the bathroom.

She can't tell who passes her as she bursts through the door sobbing, blinded by her tears and on the verge of complete hysterics. Standing in the back of the room grabbing paper towels, she keeps her back to the door as she hears it open, not wanting to face anyone and knowing she's going to be the pathetic laughing stock come Monday.

Allie cautiously puts her hands on Lea's shoulders. "What's the matter?"

"Don't ask," Lea whispers, her body shuttering from her weeping. "How'd you know I was in here?"

"I was coming to talk to you, and I saw you get up and tear off this way. You still haven't answered me. Why are you so upset? Did Dave say something?"

Lea shakes her head back and forth. "Did you notice who else was sitting around there?" she sputters quietly between sobs.

"No. Not really. I found your name and went to get you."

"Amanda."

"Oh. My. God. You've got to be joking." Behind Lea's back Allie waves towards Gail and mouths for her to go get Ms. Kertz, the other faculty sponsor and chaperone.

Lea turns to face Allie, still sobbing uncontrollably, her voice tinged with anger and disbelief, "Do I look like I'm joking? Do you think I'd be in here crying my eyes out if it was anybody else other than her and the entourage of cool..." Lea motions quotation marks in the air as she infuses the word cool with indignation and contempt, "people that have never failed to let me know how much I don't fit in in this place for the past four years? This kind of sick, perverse humor is beyond what I consider funny."

"I'm sorry. I know you're not joking. How could anyone put you two anywhere near each other? I thought the whole school knew you two don't get along."

"Apparently not. What evil karmic nightmare did I set in motion to deserve this? The last year hasn't been enough of an emotional beating? Tonight has to go horrifically wrong from step one? Can't anything work out at all?" Lea turns her back as another wave of sobs grips her and she hears the door begin to open once more.

Ms. Kertz crosses the small room to the join the young ladies in the corner. "What's wrong?" She asks sincerely concerned.

Allie does her best to relate the situation while Lea tries feebly to regain some composure.

"Everything, but the big issue right now is that there's been a major seating mistake." Allie rubs her hands up and down Lea's arms, trying to offer her all the support she can.

"What do you mean?" Ms. Kertz is obviously confused by how a seating snafu could cause this kind of break down.

Emerald has both arms wrapped around Thistle trying to protect her from the dancing flames and shadows of fear, anxiety, panic and horror that are trying to grab at them both. Their hoods blow off, leaving their faces unprotected from their whipping hair. Thistle's soft blond curls entangle with Emerald's auburn waves and thrash wildly at their faces. "Raven, help me! I can't do this without you. We need you."

Freed of her covert containment, Raven leaps up and rushes to aid Emerald and stave off the onslaught. She swishes her cloak over both Emerald and Thistle. It grows to encase them completely, allowing the flames, smoke and shadows to reach only her. She stands steadfast, granting Emerald the time to calm the terrified child. Raven's cloak shifts to and fro as Emerald hushes and rocks the young one in her arms. Raven appears unfazed as the fire and haze swirls around her, attacking her just as it had the others, trying to reach beyond her robes, blowing her hood, and letting her own onyx locks welt her pale complexion, the silver tinsel highlight strands flashing against the light of the flames.

Allie continues the story to Ms. Kertz, "We were all supposed to be seated at the same table. I turned the request into Mr. Peters myself. Somehow something got screwed up and Lea got moved. The problem being that she is now seated with some people that will make tonight a less than pleasant experience. On top of everything else that's gone wrong getting here, it's just the last straw."

"I'm sure it's not that bad," Ms. Kertz smiles, thinking she can diffuse a simple teenage over reaction.

Thistle whimpers, "She doesn't get it. She's not going to help. I wanna go home."

Lea chokes on her words, "Don't worry about it, Allie. Can you go ask Dave if he will take me home? I just want to go home. He's got a party to go to with my sister anyway. I can't do this. I just can't...." Lea's voice fades into silence and her tears continue to roll down her face, effectively washing away her sister's careful artistry.

With that all the spectators' mouths drop. This is obviously worse than Ms. Kertz had realized. She takes Allie and pulls her a step back. Gail takes Allie's place trying to support and console their friend, whispering to her, "I'm sorry, Lea. I'm so sorry."

In hushed tones, Ms. Kertz presses Allie for more

details, hoping to keep the conversation between them, but the acoustics of the bathroom don't lend aid to her intent, "Is she serious? Do you think she really would rather leave than sit with whoever she's near? Who could really be that bad? I'm obviously missing something here. What's going on?"

Allie nods her head in positive acknowledgement. "Yeah, she'll leave. Yes, it's that bad, and I wouldn't blame her or try to stop her. May I speak frankly?"

"Please do."

"How well do you know Lea?"

"She's in my class, and it's a small school, but that's about it."

"You know what she's been through with her mom then? And John?"

"Everybody does, but what does that have to do with any of this?"

"Short version... John was supposed to be here. He's not. Her mom told her she had to bring her sister if she didn't find a date. She didn't have anyone 'til three days ago, acquired by her sister, and it's a long list that she asked. Then she gets here, and all of her friends that wanted to sit with her are at one table, and she's across the room."

"I can see how that's disappointing, but that doesn't explain this," Ms. Kertz raises her hand towards Lea. The door opens behind her. The looks on the faces of the girls trying to come in is a mix between shock and curiosity. Ms. Kertz waves them out and points for them to use the other restroom down the hall.

"Do you also know Amanda Carter?" Allie resumes their whispered conversation.

At the mention of Amanda's name the dark swirling around Raven intensifies and assaults her. She circles down and wraps herself around Emerald and Thistle, ensuring they can't be

*struck. The shadows slash at her arms and back, ripping her cloak
and leaving slices across her skin. The cuts slowly bubble with
blood, but Raven doesn't move from her pose. She stays silent with
the exception of a small groan when they inflict a deep gash down
the full length of her arm, shoulder to wrist, but she just tightens
her hold around the huddled lump beneath her robes.*

"Yes," Ms. Kertz whispers back.

"How well do Lea and Amanda get along?"

"From my understanding, they aren't best friends, but
they do have a class or two together, don't they?"

"I don't know that there's anyone that Lea likes less
than Amanda with the exception of her own sister. There
was something about Amanda disrespecting Lea's Mom and
quite honestly, Lea's never forgiven her for it."

"Oh."

"Now she's supposed to spend the next few hours
sitting with Amanda and her friends, whom she's never
been acknowledged by, so tonight she has no expectation
that it will be any different than any other day. She gets to
watch them laugh, smile, have a good time, feel ostracized
some more and be reminded how everything she had hoped
for tonight didn't happen. Sounds like a great time, doesn't
it? I'd want to leave to."

Ms. Kertz looks over Allie towards Lea and Gail.
"Wait here. Don't let her go yet. Let me see what I can do.
Gail, can you come with me?" Gail leaves with Ms. Kertz.

Allie returns to her friend, who's finally running out
of tears. Her body has ceased convulsing with sobs, and her
breath is coming more regularly and less in gasps. Allie
grabs some toilet paper and hands it to Lea so she can blow
her nose. "Here. It's slightly softer than the paper towels."
Lea smirks and gives a half chuckle.

The darkness is pulling away as Raven again stands,

releasing her two charges. Emerald takes note of the wounds and the blood that now flows from her companion, her look offering compassion and her yearning to help, but Raven tilts her fingers up warding her off. She nods towards Thistle who still faces Emerald and has not seen the toll Raven has paid for her protections. Emerald nods her understanding and turns her attentions to the young girl, keeping her focused away from the flowing crimson liquid.

Raven closes her eyes, replaces her hood, hiding the pink welts across her face, and concentrates hard. The cloth of her cloak begins moving back together, reconnecting itself, hiding the evidence of what really happened. Only now can the lines of her robes be seen for what they really are... scars, ripped and sealed, torn and sewn, over and over, crisscrossing and creating an intriguing texture, until the realization hits of what they really are and where they really come from.

Although the cloth is returned to its seemingly original appearance, the truth of why lies beneath remains as a single drop of blood falls from her fingertip. Emerald notices and reaches behind Thistle to point to the drop, silently alerting Raven to the offending spot. Raven bends and clears it by wiping it into the backside of her hem. She ceases further exposure by pressing her sleeves against the gashes beneath them, letting the cloth absorb the fluid and further conceal her secrets.

Emerald disguises her motion towards Raven by grabbing Thistle's hood and lifting it back up, leaving her face partially exposed. Emerald pulls her own back into place, then reaches back to smooth the little girl's hair. She wipes Thistle's tear away, "Shhhh... We're okay. See. Ms. Kertz will fix things. Everything's going to be fine."

Thistle grabs Raven's arm, "Stay with us. Please."

Emerald's eyes pop open wide, and she starts to grab at Thistle's hand to get her to release Raven, knowing what lies *beneath the cloth just below her little hand. Raven sets her jaw and glares at Emerald, who retracts her reflexive attempt.*

Refusing to wince or cry out at the pain, Raven forces a small smile across her face and nods reassuringly at the little girl, "Of course. I'll be right here." Her voice is softer than usual and gives away no hint of the truth. "One way or another, things will work out. Worst case scenario, we'll leave. We can still go out with everyone later. It'll be fine, Wee One." Raven lifts her arm to run her fingers along Thistle's cheek, getting her to release her grip on her gashed arm without suspicion.

"Come sit with me," Emerald takes Thistle's hand and leads her over to the vined bench. Thistle looks back, ready to grab at Raven again if she doesn't come with, but Raven places her hand on Thistle's shoulder and walks with them.

Lea blows her nose hard, folds the toilet tissue and blows again. "Not real lady-like, huh? If Ginger knew about this, she'd kill me. I probably look like crap."

"You'd think so, but it's not really that bad, and probably, but I don't plan on telling her. It's a good thing you got your pictures taken already." Allie grabs a paper towel and dampens it with cold water. "You are a bit flushed though. Here." She wrings out the towel and places it on the back of Lea's neck.

"Well, that's one thing that's happened in my favor. Can I have another one for my face?"

"Sure," Allie preps a second towel and hands it over, "but only if you don't wash off all your remaining make up."

"There's still some left?" Lea presses the damp towel lightly against her reddened face, feeling the heat from her cheeks warm the towel, then wiping it down her neck and chest.

"Surprisingly yes."

S. Weary

"Ginger must have spackled me thicker than I thought."

"Where's your purse? Do you have anything to touch you up a bit?"

"It's at my seat, and I'm sure Ginger threw something in there, but I didn't pay attention as to what."

Just then Ms. Kertz and Gail returned.

"How are we doing in here?" Ms. Kertz asked.

"Little better," Lea answers.

"Good. Lea, we moved you to the edge table next to yours, Allie. All your stuff is already there. Will that work for you to stay? You'll have the table to yourselves, but that's the best I could do." Ms. Kertz watches intently, hoping her solution has resolved the crisis.

"Yes, thank you. I'm sorry to be such a bother."

"Things happen. I'm just glad we found a way to fix it." With that, Ms. Kertz nods at the girls and turns to leave. She stops at the door and quickly adds, "You will be coming back out soon, right?"

"Just as soon as we can make her presentable again," Allie pipes up. "Gail, can you go grab her purse, and mine, please?"

"Sure. Be right back. I'm so sorry, Lea." Gail turns to the door. Ms. Kertz nods, and they both leave.

Lea looks in the mirror and begins wiping away the smeared mascara, her cheeks still flushed a light red, and her eyes not nearly as blood shot as she was expecting.

"What is it?" Allie asks.

"What's what?" Lea sniffles and turns to get more tissue.

"Something's on your mind. What is it?" Allie has already stepped in a stall and is retrieving the tissue.

"Why does Gail keep apologizing? None of this is her

fault. She's not the one responsible for this fiasco." Lea blows her nose again.

Allie looks down, diverting her eyes anywhere but at Lea's. She bites her lip.

"What? What do you know?" Lea knows Allie's keeping something from her. "What is Gail feeing so guilty about?"

"Gail didn't do anything. It was Andy."

"Rook? What's he got to do with this?"

"You're finally back together. Try not to get mad..."

"Go on..."

"Rook's the one that had you moved from the table."

"He what!?!" Lea's eyes harden and glare at her friend and then up through the door, seeking the vile, back-stabbing, little snot that was responsible for the latest diabolical twist to her nightmare.

Raven snarls and growls, "I'm going to kill him! I'm going to rip his arms off and beat him with them! I'm going to kick his ass so hard he'll taste my toenail polish for years!"

"Raven, try to calm down," Emerald stares, wondering if Raven will still be able to hear reason, or is she already past that line into rage. "You can't do anything to him without destroying Gail's night and possibly DiAna and Nick too. They all came together, remember?"

"I. Don't. Care."

Thistle scoots closer to Emerald. "You're frightening Thistle," Emerald states.

"No, she's not," Thistle adds, "I'm just staying out of her way." She grins innocently at Raven. "I don't like him, so I don't really care if she beats him up."

"Love this girl." Raven smiles evilly and blows Thistle a kiss.

"Not good. Not helping. Not healthy....." Emerald

remarks, more to herself than the audience she knows isn't really listening to her anyway. "You're over eighteen! You're an adult! You can be arrested for assault and battery, and you don't look good in orange." This seems to pause Raven for a moment, allowing Lea to hear what Allie has to say.

Lea focuses back on her friend as Allie speaks, "I found Mr. Peters after we found your seats. Apparently, when he realized that we had too many people at our table, he asked Andy who should be bumped."

"Of all the people he could have asked, he goes to the only one that would have suggested this, the only one that didn't specifically want to sit with me. Seriously? That little twerp!" Lea's cheeks flush again, but this time no tears will be following.

"That's why Gail keeps saying she's sorry. He's her date. If she hadn't agreed to come with him, he wouldn't be at the table, and it wouldn't have happened."

"Not her fault, but I'd really like to..." Lea is interrupted by Gail returning with the purses hopefully containing everything needed for emergency reconstruction of Lea's mask.

Gail sees the look of fury on Lea's face and realizes she now knows who was responsible. She opens her mouth to apologize again, but Lea cuts her off. "Don't." Gail shuts down and looks at the floor, thinking Lea is justifiably angry with her as well. "It's not your fault. You didn't do it, and it's not your place to apologize to me for anything." Gail lifts her head to face Lea again. "If Mr. Peters had asked you, would you have told him to bump me?"

"No," Gail replies.

"Then we have no issue. Thanks for helping me out though. Can I have my purse?"

Gail hands it over with Allie's. They both open them

and start pulling out what they have to work with.

"All that being well and good, I'd still warn Rook to stay away from her tonight," Allie rolls her eyes towards Gail as a polite hint, "and maybe 'til graduation too."

"He wants to apologize," Gail adds.

Lea's head turns slowly to look at Gail like the fifty caliber tourette guns on a World War Two battleship taking aim. Allie catches Lea's reaction in the mirror and quickly faces Gail, "Not a real good idea. Better if he stays out of striking distance." Gail nods anxiously, understanding.

"So what do we have to work with?" Allie changes the subject.

"Mascara, lip-gloss, and powder, but no eye shadow, blush or eye liner," Lea voices the inventory.

"You don't need blush, and, if we had either shadow or liner, we could skip the other," Allie states. "Gail, do you have anything?"

"I think I have some eye liner, but it's black," Gail perks up, feeling she may be able to help.

"Perfect!" Both Allie and Lea say in unison.

"Hey, can you tell Carl to move our place settings over by Lea and Dave?" Allie throws out as Gail rushes out the door to retrieve the liner. Turning back to her best friend, she adds, "That way you guys won't have to sit by yourselves."

"Thanks." Lea smiles, finally feeling like the night may be salvageable.

They go to work replastering as best they can into a presentable look, powder to even her color out a bit, gloss disguising the fact that her lips were uncharacteristically red, dabbing any moisture off her existing shadow and realizing it had come through with minimal damage. The coal black liner fully surrounding her eyes, which Ginger would not have, and has never, approved of but also fit both Lea's personality and her current state of mind, and lastly some mascara to replace what had been nearly completely washed away by Lea's recent attempt to rechannel Niagara Falls through her eyes.

"Well?" Lea faces her friends for examination.

"Not bad," Allie critiques. "If I hadn't been here with you, I wouldn't be able to tell anything had happened."

"You look beautiful," Gail adds.

Lea smiles at them, albeit unsure how honest Gail is being considering her feelings of guilt about it all, "Then let's get out of here." The three of them leave and head back to their tables along the far wall.

When they pass by Ms. Kertz, Lea pauses, nods, and quietly thanks her once again. Ms. Kertz returns the smile, and very quietly murmurs, "You're welcome." Allie hesitates her step to stay with Lea, also giving Ms. Kertz a grateful smile before the three young ladies continue on.

As they approach the tables, Rook stands to address them as they pass. Gail grabs his arm trying to return him to his seat next to her, but, in his utter oblivion, he misses the hint.

Raven clenches her fists and grinds her teeth. "Emerald, this kid's got a death wish." Emerald pulls Thistle close to her as the little girl watches with whimsical anticipation.

Allie gets his attention by quietly telling him, "Andy, don't. Just let her by."

Still baffled, confused, and having no clue what lies beneath Lea's barely contained exterior he begins to speak.

Emerald shifts Thistle to her other side, putting herself as a block between her and Raven in case the boiling rage erupts beyond control and Raven loses the ability to see what she is swinging at.

"He's a masochist! He's begging me to just punch him in

the face!" Heat fumes off of Raven like the rippling waves off the pavement in the middle of August.

"I just wanted to..." is all Rook can get before Lea interrupts him.

"Get.... Away.... From me," Lea growls in a guttural almost demonic tone that no one else can hear except Rook and Allie. The entire company of both tables, including Dave, is however witnessing the penetrating glare of frenzied savagery. Lea's hands shake at her side as adrenaline courses through her, feeding the violent rampage Raven aches to release upon the feeble insect standing before Lea.

Allie cocks her eyebrow, slightly amused, but not completely surprised by the altercation. The corner of her lip raises as Andy steps away, submissively dropping his eyes, shrinking and finding his seat.

Preoccupied by maintaining her own self-control, Lea is incognizant of the looks of shock on her friends' faces, never having seen her that angry before but all suspecting what they just witnessed was there, lying in wait. Allie disguises Lea's shaking hands by grabbing one in her own and glancing down for Lea to grab hold of her purse with the other. They walk around to their own table where Dave and Carl are already seated.

Skirting around Nick, Allie and Lea hear him whisper to DiAna, "What did I miss?" DiAna grabs his leg under the table trying unsuccessfully to get him to drop his inquiry. "It had to be something good 'cause you all got real quiet, and I swear the temperature in here just shifted." Allie snickers at Lea as DiAna begins whispering feverishly in his ear and they cross the point of hearing any further comments.

Carl stands to pull out Allie's chair. Not to be embarrassed by a kid three years his junior, Dave quickly stands, but is too late for any further gentlemanly acts as Lea is already pulling out her own chair and seating herself. They all sit back down.

Dave leans over towards Lea noticing the twitching in her fingers under the table. "You okay?"

"Yes, I'm fine. Sorry about all that, and thank you for moving over here."

"Do I want to know what all that was about?" Dave shoots a look towards Rook.

"It was nothing."

Dave nods his head up and down, "That's a pretty intense nothing," and looks down at Lea's hands.

Emerald steps over to Raven, whose breathing is just shy of hyperventilating. "You've got to calm down."

"I'm trying. It just might take longer than you'd like." *Raven closes her eyes and tries to concentrate on slowing her breaths.*

Lea glances over to Rook, who still doesn't risk even glimpsing in her direction. "He's the one that had us bumped from the table, and thusly banished me to the hell that could have been, also he's the only one here that would have chosen me to be the one to be moved from this group."

"Ah. I see." Dave reaches over and lays his hand on top of Lea's, holding it there 'til the shaking and twitching stops. "Everything else okay now?"

"Everything's fine." Lea smiles politely and turns her attention to Carl and Allie, finally taking notice of their location among the row of unoccupied tables against the wall. They are all covered with a tablecloth, but are otherwise bare. Still, it is a marked improvement from the adorned previous placement, and, with Allie and Carl there, it is just lovely.

Lea notices a couple approaching out of the corner of

her eye. Brian and Lauren have arrived. They are a couple rows over and up but meandered through to chat with everyone. Lea smiles and waves and pops up for quick hugs, but returns to her seat as Brian talks with Andy. She glances around the room, noticing how much fuller it is than when they first arrived, almost all the tables are at least partially filled now and people are milling around and chatting.

Lea's stomach growls. She looks around to see if anyone else notices. She grabs her water glass and takes a drink. It falls to the bottom of her stomach like a cold block of lead falling down a well.

"Ugh! I hate water!" Raven complains.

"How can you hate water? You swim," Emerald counters.

"Put a couple drops of chlorine in here, and I may not mind it so much." Raven shoots back.

Emerald shakes her head and offers Thistle her coloring supplies back. The young lass leaps at the offering and once again spreads herself across the floor and amuses herself with her hues and tints and imaginings.

Lea grimaces at the fluid. Allie turns to Carl, "Come with me." Without a word, Carl obediently follows.

"Where you going?" Lea inquires.

"We'll be right back," Allie is already taking off towards the hall door.

"What's that about?" Dave wonders out loud.

"Haven't got a clue. With her it could be anything." Lea suffers another drink of water, hoping to ward off any further stomach disturbances before dinner starts.

"Scott Logan is supposed to be here somewhere if you wanted to go find him."

"I know. Already saw him while you were in the bathroom."

"Oh." Lea and Dave sit in silence, people watching

for the few minutes until their tablemates return, a member of the catering staff following them.

"What was all that about?" Lea asks.

"You not liking water and being hungry." Allie retorts with obvious self-satisfaction.

The uniformed young man places a basket of rolls and butter on the table and walks away. Lea hadn't noticed before that all the tables had two such baskets next to their centerpieces. Allie checks behind to see if her former table was taking notice of her actions. Appeased that they are clueless, she and Carl start pulling out cans of soda and placing them on the table.

"I wasn't sure what you liked, Dave, so we grabbed a couple options."

"Anything you got works for me."

"Allie, where'd you get these? I didn't see a vending machine." Lea asks being handed a cola, grateful that her friend is one of those people that can just 'get things' no matter the circumstances.

"Just gotta know who to ask…, and that usually means someone that's working, not the ones organizing." Allie smirks, proud of herself and her abilities of acquirement.

Raven beams with appreciation, "She has got to be the coolest girl I know."

"Undoubtedly," Emerald agrees and goes back to nibbling on her grapes.

Rolls passed and buttered, and water set aside for the much tastier bubbly refreshments. They all are content to sit back and wait for the festivities to commence.

~ *Dinner or Dancing* ~

It wasn't that long before the catering staff began
passing out the dinner plates. The change in seating proves
to be an upgrade and offers certain unexpected benefits, as
they are one of the first tables being served. First came a
French onion soup with grated cheese on top, tossed salad of
mixed greens, followed by filet mignon with garlic potatoes
and steamed vegetables.

Lea is pleasantly surprised as their meals seemed
both properly cooked and still warm, which is often not the
case in large catered events like this. Not fond of overly rare
meat, her beef was well done yet still moist, and the potatoes
and vegies hadn't begun to cool at all. Nobody at the table
voices any complaints making the dining a real pleasure.

The DJ begins some hushed music during the dining,
reminding everyone that this is a dance and there is more to
come. There are only certain parts of the country that can
combine Cher, Garth Brooks, Chicago, Rush, Reba McEntire,
Prince, Sinead O'Conner, Restless Heart, and others into a
seamless stream of musical accompaniment to a meal and

still have it make sense. This would be one of those places. Time passes with no real measure other than the changing of songs.

"Mmmm. This is actually good," Emerald compliments the meal.

"I know. I'm shocked." Raven stammers.

"Do you think Allie said something when she talked to the staff?" Emerald watches her friend eating, trying to read if she had a hand in the well-presented grub or if it was just better service than they had gotten here last year. "I hope she didn't. That would be so embarrassing. Don't enough people know about tonight already?"

"I've been wondering the same thing, but don't really care about the embarrassing part if it means somebody is trying to make this a positively memorable experience," Raven's nonchalant in her reply, focusing instead on trying to encourage Lea to take another bite of her filet mignon.

"See things are turning out better already. Mind if get a couple bites of salad before you fill me up with meat and potatoes?"

"If you insist, but I think I have room for it all. Nervous breakdowns and hysterical fits seem to burn a lot of calories, and it's going to be a long night, so I need to rebuild the energy stores."

Thistle bounces her foot with the beat, continuing her childish diversion as Depeche Mode gets laced into the musical mix.

"Yeah, I think someone has hopes of hitting the dance floor later." Emerald's tone once again lightened as she watches.

Allie breaks the silence of the table, "Your food okay?"

"Uh huh. Yours?" Lea answers.

"Not bad. I've had worse. Was it like this last year?"

"Not really. If I remember right, it was barely warm by the time we got served. What about you, Carl? You were here last year. What do you think?" Lea reaches the conversation outward.

"No idea. I've slept since then. I'm a guy. Food is food. As long as it's edible, I'll eat it," with that he shovels another bite of potatoes in his mouth.

The girls look over to Dave, "Don't ask me," he volunteers before they can pose any question. "I wasn't here, and he's right in that, as guys, we don't pay attention to that stuff. If it's edible, we eat." Dave snickers to himself as he takes his next bite, keeping himself from saying something he obviously shouldn't.

"Ewwww.... How gross! No doubt he just jumped to some disgusting thought about my sister," Raven shudders at the possibility of what might be running through her escort's mind.

Allie seems to jump to the same thought as Raven. Both Lea and Allie throw looks of disapproval in Dave's direction.

"What?!?" Dave defends himself from the visual attack.

"No need to make it pervy," Lea barks softly.

At this Carl's head pops up from his meal, extremely curious to what it was that he missed. "Huh?"

"I didn't say anything," Dave's attempt to shield himself from the accusation is weak at best, further convincing the girls that his thoughts were more than slightly sliding in the gutter.

"You didn't have to. Your chuckle betrayed you." Lea rests her case.

Allie turns to Carl, "And don't go getting any ideas from his bad influence."

Carl looks at Allie, then to Dave and back to Allie completely unaware what he's being accused of or what's going on. "Okay?" He focuses back on his meal.

"In my defense ladies, IF I had been implying something inappropriate, wouldn't you both have to have had the same thought in order to catch me in it, so doesn't that make you just as guilty as I am?" Dave thinks he's gotten the upper hand on the two assailants.

Lea looks to Allie, they share a short conversation without speaking before addressing him again.

"Speaking hypothetically of course, IF we potentially had that same thought as you, and we aren't admitting that we did, neither of us expressed it or reacted to it," Lea begins.

Dave stops and looks at them dumbfounded.

"We didn't snicker," Allie finishes the idea.

"Does it really matter if he's thinking that?" Emerald asks Raven. "Ginger's not going to let it happen."

"True, and this meal and his fantasies might be his only pay off for his good deed in saving me, but I really don't need to know he's thinking it. I have a very creative imagination and that's a picture I REALLY don't want drawn." Raven replies.

A rather mischievous grin crosses Dave's face, "So Lea, hypothetically speaking, doesn't that also imply that you have some personal knowledge or experience to draw from in reaching that same conclusion?"

Lea blushes and forcibly swallows her food. Carl, having taken the last bite effectively clearing his plate, grabs his soda to wash it down, trying to act as if he hasn't been actively following the conversation to determine what he missed.

Dave continues, "Just funny to me because I was always under the impression that percussionists were better with their hands."

Lea's eyes flare open wide. Allie sucks in a vacuum of air and squeezes her lips shut to stifle the laughter that she knows Lea will not appreciate. Carl can't balance his amused chortles and the soda he's thankfully only sipped from as it comes flying back out through his nose, spraying onto his recently emptied dinner plate.

Allie can't contain her laughter further and a series of guffaws escapes, her stomach spasms with her outburst. Dave joins her, thoroughly pleased with the surprising reaction. Even Lea's embarrassment is set aside by the impromptu entertainment.

Carl grabs his napkin and attempts to apologize, but the words are lost in the commotion.

"Good thing you'd finished that already," Dave tries to bring some composure back to the table which is now drawing attention from the volume.

Carl wipes his face and lays his napkin over his plate to try and hide the evidence. The catering staff appears and reaches for the plates. Before clearing Carl's away the gentleman asks, "Did you want to keep your napkin?"

"No, thank you." Carl respectfully answers causing everyone else to resume their chuckling.

Their waiter completes clearing the table and moves on to the next one, focusing on quickly and quietly making room for dessert.

DiAna taps Lea on the shoulder, "How long are we planning to stay?"

Allie turns with Lea, curious to her answer, "Well, they'll be some dancing and then the coronation. They put that near the end to keep people from leaving too soon. I think we're planning to stay at least that long. You don't have to if you really don't want to."

"That's fine. Just curious is all," DiAna returns to her own table and conversations.

"So do you even know who's in the court?" Allie

leans in whispering her query.

"No idea." Lea returns the hushed answer, "but I also don't want to think about what they are planning if they are already talking about leaving before dessert's even been served, especially since they rode down with Rook. I didn't think Gail was really that cozy with him."

"I don't think she is. You really think that's what DiAna meant?"

"Let's just say I wouldn't be surprised."

"Really? I didn't think she'd been dating Nick that long. Are they dating at all?"

"I don't think that's the point."

Allie leans back as they are serve chocolate mousse. She glances over at Carl, "Think you can get this down the right way?"

"I'll do my best," Carl takes a careful bite.

As the catering staff begins their last clearing of the tables, the lights above the dance floor dim, and both the volume and beat increase. The floor fills with shadowed bodies moving, swaying, and gyrating to the rhythm.

Lea's toe taps to the beat, as the music shifts from song to song. She watches Allie out of the corner of her eye.

"Okay, so I've found an issue with my best friend. Her one outstanding flaw," Raven critiques.

"And that is?" Emerald encourages the thought.

"She doesn't dance."

"That's not true. She dances. How many after game dances did I go to and hung out with her? She danced there."

"Good point... Which means she's not dancing now because she doesn't want to encourage Carl, and that still doesn't help our cause."

"But Carl has never danced before, why would he start now?"

"Because he likes her..."

The pulse slows as an inspiring Chicago ballad pipes through the room. Allie squirms in her chair, turning her back towards Carl. He slumps in his seat. Dave watches the dark figures swaying, apparently oblivious to the slight.

"Wow! That was subtle. You win Emerald. Even I'm starting to feel bad for this guy." Raven marvels at the extent Allie is going to make sure not to encourage any crossed wires.

"So are we still going to your house first after this?" Allie feigns planning so as not to have to acknowledge Carl's crushed hopes.

"As far as I'm aware, yes." Lea looks to Dave, including him in the conversation. "Did I hear right that you're meeting Ginger at some party later?"

"Yeah," Dave is surprised that Lea knows about it.

"So yeah, he'll drop me off there. I'll grab my clothes, and the three of us can head out to the diner."

"Mind if we join you?" DiAna is standing between Lea and Allie, holding Nick's hand, guiding him behind her.

Lea looks past her friend to see the rest of the table has abandoned them to the dance floor. "Sure. Dave, Carl, scoot down a seat." The two couples part down the middle allowing DiAna and Nick to sit between them. Nick hooks his arm over DiAna's chair and around her shoulders as a guide to her position in relation to himself.

Lea returns to the previous conversation, "Anybody see Brian lately? We should remind him that we're all planning on following him from the diner."

Nick answers her first, "Well, considering I've never seen Brian in the first place, I think it's safe to say no." Dave and Carl snicker at Nick, but the girls just roll their eyes.

"He and Lauren were over there just a second ago," Allie peers through the tables seeking a reason to jump and run at any opportunity.

Lea puts her hand on Nick's leg, leaning over to gently scold her friend, "Stop it. We'll find them later. No rush."

Nick puts his arm around Lea before she can sit back up, "Hey Di, maybe we should have ridden with them." He tilts his head towards Lea and Dave.

"That might get really cramped considering it's only a two-seater," Dave douses the suggestion.

"Oooo... Even better, a threesome in the passenger's seat." Nick excites himself with the idea. Dave and Carl chuckle.

"I don't think so," Lea sits back up and out of Nick's grasp.

"Ah, come on, give me a chance. I might surprise you," Nick goads her.

Lea slides her hand under Nick's, "Now tell me why I think that might be a complete waste of your time?" He feels over her fingers and finds her ring.

"What a way to kill a guy's fantasy," he replies.

Allie grows increasingly antsy in her position. The six of them glued to their chairs as another set of tunes plays through.

"Okay, so I've got to know, how did you two meet?" Allie asks DiAna.

Nick pipes up quickly, "She got set up on a blind date, but didn't know that also meant her date would be blind."

DiAna turns to her, "We bumped into each other on the strip."

"And I enjoyed what I felt," Nick pops in again.

DiAna elbows him in the ribs. "Truth is we have some mutual friends out there that introduced us."

"Please, don't think me rude, but is there a reason you twist every comment into a sexual thing, Nick?" Lea pointedly asks him.

"Isn't that what you were expecting?" he answers.

"Expecting? I have no idea what you're talking about," she's perplexed by his retort.

"The thing about being blind is your hearing really does improve."

"I've heard that," Lea acknowledges.

"But you must have forgotten that little tidbit when you ladies were discussing why Di was asking when you planned on leaving," Nick reveals.

Allie gasps and covers her mouth.

Lea drops her head, "I'm sorry. That was rude."

"I'm just curious, since you've never met me before, why would you jump to that conclusion?"

"Wasn't you at all. It's Di," Lea admits. "You have no way to know this, but she keeps looking at you like the whip cream on top of an ice cream sundae."

Dave injects, "All you need is a cherry on top."

"Please, somebody tell me that Di's dress is red." Nick utters hopefully.

The original foursome all crack up laughing.

"Actually, it is," DiAna answers.

"And now so are her cheeks," Lea adds.

Nick leans towards DiAna giving her a light kiss on her temple. "Any chance I can get a soda that I know you guys are hiding over here?" Nick asks of Allie and Carl. "Might help her cool down a bit."

"I think that can be arranged." Allie gets up relieved at her excuse to avoid standard Prom rituals. She nods her head for Carl to come with, and he gets up and follows.

"So what do you do, Nick?" Lea asks curiously.

"Right now I volunteer at a suicide hotline," he's serious and sincere, "but I've thought about going into counseling."

"Really?" Lea props her face on her hand intrigued and concentrating completely on him.

"Yeah, but it'll be harder for me because I'm not able to read body language, which can be a huge part of understanding what people are really trying to express, so I'm also considering maybe being a guidance counselor at a blind school."

"That's why he's here with me," DiAna breaks Lea's focus. "He thinks he can fix me."

Lea snickers, "So you brought him to a gathering of the hopeless cases to prove that can't be done?"

"Something like that," DiAna laughs.

"That's okay," Nick drops the seriousness from his face. "My back up plan is to offer my services as a breast implant inspector."

Dave turns his attention away from the dance floor, "Let me know how I can get in on that."

"Well, like any skill, you have to be sure you're properly trained," Nick tightens his arm around DiAna, squeezing her close to him and causing her to flush bright red again.

Lea smiles, but tries hard not to laugh, relieved that she isn't the only one being picked on tonight, "Hey Di, at least when your date embarrasses you, you match your dress."

Allie and Carl return, hands and pockets full of the second round of contraband beverages. They pass them around the table, giving everyone the opportunity to quench their thirst with the bubbly potables.

"We're going to have to do something to help Carl out,"

Emerald plots.

"*That would be so much easier if Dave would dance with me just once, but I don't think that's going to happen.*" Raven is obviously disappointed in her escort's obliviousness.

"*He might yet. I know he can dance. I've seen him.*"

"*I know that, and you know that, and, if it was Ginger sitting here, we wouldn't be having this conversation, so I'm not going to hold my breath and turn blue over it. Whatever you plan on doing, you better get on it. I think it's slowing again.*"

When the second slow set begins, Lea recognizes the beginning piano flare. She turns to Dave, "Excuse me." She calmly gets up and heads off to the bathroom.

"What's this one about?" Dave asks turning towards Allie and Carl.

Allie listens a moment. "Tommy Page... Oh..." The realization hits her. "This is the song she sang to her mom last fall before everything spiraled and she went in the coma. I'll be back." Allie and DiAna take off after Lea. They catch up at the restroom door.

"You okay?" Lea is startled by Allie's voice behind her.

"I'm fine. What are you two doing here?"

"I heard the song... I thought...." Allie drops her eyes.

"Honestly, she thought when you got up and left that you were freaking out," DiAna states bluntly.

"No.... I just have to pee. Didn't think I needed any help with that." Lea excuses herself into a stall.

"You had a strange look on your face," Allie justifies her reaction.

"I recognized the song. That's all. No meltdown, but since you're here anyway, maybe we can talk about you cutting Carl a little slack?" DiAna snickers at the turn of events.

Allie whines, "Ugh. Why would I want to do that?"

"Because he's your date, and he's nice," DiAna backs Lea up.

"But I don't want him to get the wrong idea," Allie tries defending herself. "You guys know he likes me."

"You've made sure he's perfectly clear that you don't think of him that way. We're all perfectly clear on that." Lea steps out of the stall and washes her hands. "Now we're going back out there and you're going to dance with him at least once. Clear?"

Allie whines and groans, "Fine."

"Somebody ought to enjoy tonight, and, since it's not going to be me, and, obviously, it's not you, at least Carl can have a pleasant time."

Back at the table, Lea winks at Carl and gives Allie a light nudge. DiAna sits quickly, getting out of Allie's way. Allie rolls her eyes, but holds out her hand. Carl leaps at his chance and leads her to the floor before the set ends.

Dave doesn't follow suit, so Lea sits back down. "Was your Prom really that bad or were you just saying that to try and make me feel better?"

"No lie. It was that bad. This is better."

"Even with the extra theatrics?"

"Yep."

"I have a theory on that. I think it's a matter of balance," Nick begins. "For everyone that has a good time at a Prom, someone else has to have an equally horrible time, and, if you're lucky, it's not within the same couple."

"Well, that would be Allie and Carl right now," DiAna chuckles. She and Lea look over watching the mismatched couple dance. Carl's grinning from ear to ear, but as they rotate around, Allie glares at her friends that orchestrated this moment. "They remind me of the conflicting drama masks."

"Ladies, can you please explain to me why in the world, if she doesn't like him, did she agree to come with him?" Nick asks.

"I'm curious about that too," Dave's interest spikes.

"It's my fault," Lea tells them. "But, in my defense, I didn't know she was going to go into overdrive to keep him at bay."

"That doesn't really explain why," Nick pursues further.

DiAna fields his inquiry. "It's a special occasion for our warped and dark leader to your right, and we are all her minions. Allie being the highest ranking minion among us HAD to be in attendance, but she's not old enough, which makes Carl's crush incredibly convenient."

Lea protests, "I am not your leader, and I don't have minions! Where do you come up with this stuff?

"Like it or not, people are drawn to you," DiAna continues.

"I am not that popular," Lea persists in her refusal of the description.

"Well, of course not. Popular people lure in people trying to be popular and craving status by association. You don't care about status or social position and thusly collect a following of rejects seeking to be free of those concerns and labels and to have your confidence in shrugging them off. You're Queen of the Rejects. Deal with it." DiAna explains.

"Now that explains a lot," Nick buys into DiAna's version.

"Whatever. You're crazy. I've never aspired to this role you're claiming I have." Lea brushes it off.

"If they had the slightest clue of what I really felt or

thought, they would be immensely disappointed," Raven weighs in.

"Maybe," Emerald says, "but you have to admit that looking at it from her point of view, that's how they see you."

"Even so, it's a position I've been forced into by my own lack of acceptance by... well everyone. I didn't choose this isolation, and I really DON'T see myself as a role model for anyone." Raven concludes.

The music resumes its quickened pace. Lea turns to watch Allie and Carl as Allie rushes back to the table, Carl lagging behind but pleased to have gotten her onto the dance floor.

"Did you guys see that?" Allie's overly excited.

"Do you all realize how many times you've asked me if I've seen something tonight?" Nick lifts his hands, palms up, helpless.

Lea pats Nick's shoulder, "Obviously not you. What did we miss?"

Carl takes his seat and lets Allie blurt out the latest twist, "Mike and Michelle were dancing and Todd walked up to them and said something. Next thing I know, all three of them are headed for the door, Todd shoves Mike and Michelle steps between them to keep them from fighting." Only after she's let it all out does she take her seat... and a breath.

"That's not good. Where are they now?" Lea asks, sliding to the edge of her chair, alert and ready to go step in if need be.

Emerald looks hard at Dave wondering if he'll come along if she has to chase them down.

"Don't count on it," Raven swats the thought away. "If need be, I've got it covered."

Allie continues, "Mr. Peters stepped in, separating

112

them, and I think Todd got kicked out. Mike and Michelle went out in the hall and Rook and Gail are out there with them now."

Carl nods in agreement confirming Allie's account of events.

"We should go check on Michelle," Emerald urges.

"Gail's got it, and I don't think it's a good idea to put me near Rook with that much adrenaline surging around us, do you?" Raven re-evaluates the scene.

Lea decides to stay at the table. "I wonder what all that was about?"

DiAna curls her lips in and bites her mouth closed tightly.

Emerald yells, pointing at DiAna, "Raven, she knows something!"

Raven examines DiAna intently, "I have a feeling she knows exactly what was behind it."

"Diii?" Lea draws out her name. "Spill it!"

DiAna hesitates.

"Your twisted leader demands it, Minion girl!" Lea adds.

DiAna cracks at the reference, "What I heard was that Michelle was out at the strip last weekend. Mike wasn't with her, and she ended up at some party where Todd was. They were both drinking, and things happened."

"Is it true?" Allie's eyes pop with eagerness at being let in on the gossip.

"I don't know." DiAna shakes her head from side to side. "I know she was on the strip. I saw her, but I didn't go to the party, so I don't know from there."

"Todd who? Who's party was it?" Nick asks her.

"Todd Delon, and I don't know the guy's name, but he drives that old GTO with the really growly engine."

DiAna answers him.

"I know that engine. I was there," Nick offers. "Todd was there with some girl, but I couldn't tell you who it was."

Dave clears his throat, alerting everyone that the subjects of their discussion were heading towards them.

Nick searches for his can and raises his drink for a toast, "To the balance of Prom and to everyone having a wonderful night thanks to our stumbles of misfortune." The sextet all grab their beverages and reach in to clink cans in a cluster around his.

Before they can say anything or inquire of their extended group, the DJ starts calling the court to the floor. Lea grabs her purse and listens with disinterest. She leans over Nick to DiAna, "Tell Allie to give him one more dance. It won't kill her. I'll meet them at my house."

As soon as the formal announcements are made, Lea turns to Dave, "Ready?"

"Sure."

Lea says quick goodbyes and reminds everyone that she'll see them at the diner. She eyes the carnations on the center of the table. Without asking, she grabs the flowers and lays them on her photo frame. She snags more flowers from an unoccupied table at the corner and adds them to her pile. Prom flowers acquired.

Lea and Dave leave for his car while the court still 'Holds on to the Night' on the dance floor.

~ *Road Hazards* ~

As Dave pulls onto the highway heading back home, Lea turns to him, "Thank you... I really do appreciate you doing this for me."

"You're welcome."

They aren't even clear of the Capital City outskirts when Dave looks down at his dash and pulls off to the side of the highway. Lea didn't feel anything, so it isn't likely a flat.

"He better not be getting any stupid ideas," Raven is not pleased with the unfolding events.

"I don't think that's the case. Look at his face. He's honestly concerned." Emerald reserves her judgment for the moment.

Thistle stretches and yawns. "Hey there, Pretty Girl. I think it's time for you to head to bed," Emerald coos. Thistle's eyes droop and fall as she nods her head in acceptance. She first hugs Emerald and then Raven and shuffles her feet off into the darkness.

"What's wrong?" Lea's curiosity pierces the silence.

"I'm not sure, but we're not going anywhere 'til I

figure it out." Dave shuts off the car and steps out. He removes his jacket and folds it over his arm. "I think I've got a spare t-shirt in the back." Lea nods understanding that he's only saying this so she doesn't think he's leaving. Dave disappears and returns in an older well-worn white tee with some design on it, but it's too dark to distinguish it. His jacket and dress shirt are both missing.

"Would you like me to leave the radio on for you?"

"Yes, please."

He turns the key and then heads back to the rear of the car again.

"Anybody else wondering if Dave is actually a serial killer?" Raven fills the boredom with her wondering.

"Really, Raven?" Emerald is exacerbated. "Let's be logical for just one second here. Let's assume for the moment that he is. How smart would it be for him to kill me? Everyone knows I am with him. How would he cover his tracks? Wouldn't he end up being the prime suspect?"

Before Raven can launch a counter debate, flashing lights catch Lea's eye. A police car is pulling up behind them, the lights bouncing off the side mirror into Lea's face, irritating her vision.

"Ah, there you go. Nothing more to worry about. Police on the scene, so Dave won't be able to pull out the murder kit he was hiding in the trunk." Emerald gloats, feeling this wins her argument and dismisses Raven's morbid train of thought.

An attractive officer, in his early to mid-twenties, knocks on Lea's window. Lowering the glass, she finds herself gazing into his mesmerizing blue-grey eyes, "Yes sir?"

"Are you alright, Miss? Everything okay?" His voice is sincere.

"With the exception of this busted hunk of metal stranding

116

me way too far from home and no way to call for help," Raven bellows.

"With me? Yes, Sir, I'm fine." Lea finds his questions odd.

"Have to make sure, Miss." He cocks a half smile at her, apparently enjoying the humor of the moment. "Let me see what I can do to get you back on your way." Officer Friendly stands and heads back to Dave.

"See, even the cop double checked that I wasn't the future mystery victim found in a ditch," Raven refuses to relinquish her train of thought.

"Huh? Yeah, sure, whatever. Did he just wink at me when he walked away? Did you see his eyes?" Emerald barely acknowledges Raven's continued tangent, instead trying to follow Officer Friendly in the mirror despite the bright flashes.

"I don't know. Maybe." Raven watches in disbelief as Emerald attempts to ogle him. "John," she states in a clear, solid tone.

Emerald's attention whips back towards Raven. "What about him?"

"Forget about him already?"

"Absolutely not! But I have a weakness for intriguing eyes and you have to admit Officer Friendly back there has unusual and intense eyes. I was just admiring them."

"If you say so, but, when you were watching him walk away, it wasn't his eyes you were looking at."

Dave opens his door, offering Lea an update, "Looks like the clutch went out. Sorry. He's gonna try contacting my parents."

"Okay," Lea's a little shocked at his willingness to go the extra step to let her know what's going on, and thankful he didn't witness her spellbound reaction to Officer Friendly. "Can I ask you something without you thinking

I'm a total moron?"

"Sure."

"How can you tell what's wrong if you haven't even popped the hood?" Lea looks out the windshield at the still closed front end.

Dave chuckles slightly, "Because it's a split engine. The clutch is in the trunk."

"Oh," Lea blushes with embarrassment, and Dave spares her any further distress by closing the door and returning to Officer Friendly.

"Raven?" Emerald called. "Was that Carl's brown van that just zipped past behind Dave?"

"That's a very good possibility."

"I can't believe they just blew by here without stopping."

"After everything else, that's unbelievable to you? I'm considering it par for the course."

"Hold that thought, Oh Negative One. Who is this pulling in front of us?"

A pearl Cadillac pulls off, then reverses to close the distance between them, and stops.

"I don't think I know anyone that would be driving that. Raven?" Emerald is stumped.

"It's a Cadillac! Obviously NOT a student's car. I'm pretty sure I would have noticed that in the student parking lot."

The driver gets out and heads back towards the stranded vehicle. The twirling lights from the police cruiser blind Lea from being able to see who it is. He's right next to the car before Lea realizes that it's Scott Logan.

"Okay, that is so not his car…," Raven protests.

Lea jumps in her seat as Scott opens her door.

"Sorry. Didn't mean to startle you. Would you like a ride home?"

"YES, PLEASE!!!" Emerald cheers and dances in a circle.

Raven rolls her eyes at the display.

"You don't mind?" Lea asks.

"Come on," Scott gives her a kind smile and offers his hand to help her out of the vehicle. Lea quickly grabs her things and gratefully accepts his assistance.

She looks over the top of the busted buggy at Dave. "My parents are already on their way, and the car still has to get towed," he states.

"Oh, okay. Well, thanks again." Lea balances her things in one arm, freeing her other hand to close the door. Glancing over at Dave again, she forces a grin. "Good night."

She walks off to the passenger side of the Cadi where Scott is holding the back door open for her, leaving Dave with his broken car, a police cruiser still flashing its lights, and Officer Friendly.

"Think his car figured out Ginger was just a tease?" Raven ponders.

"Why would you ask such a question?" Emerald is baffled by where this may be heading.

"Well, if she won't go all the way, why should it take me all the way home?"

"You are disturbed, Raven."

"Thanks," Lea drops her eyes sheepishly as she steps into the car.

"Not a problem," Scott smiles and closes the door.

As he slides in behind the wheel, Lea sees his date, Rachel sitting in front of her.

"Should I put on my seatbelt this time?" Lea asks.

"What?" Scott replies.

"This isn't the first time you've had to rescue me when I needed a ride home."

"Dad taught us never to ignore a damsel in distress,

but what does that have to do with you wearing your seatbelt?"

"Last time you told me I wouldn't need it because we were in your dad's truck and if we got in a wreck I should hope I die because if I didn't and he found out the truck got wrecked because you were taking me home, he'd kill me anyway ... and you."

Scott laughs softly, "Well, this is Rachel's dad's car, so feel free to put it on if you like."

Rachel leans over towards Scott, her head falls below Lea's line of vision, presumably lying across the front seat.

"Oh you've got to be kidding me?" Raven huffs her irritation.

"What?" Emerald doesn't follow the source of Raven's displeasure. "What's the problem?"

"Well, it's uncomfortable enough being a third wheel on their date, but now her head's in his lap. Do I really need to start drawing you pictures? Hand me Thistle's supplies. I'll paint it out for you." Raven spits through pursed lips.

"No!" Emerald gasps. "Surely not. I mean not while I'm in the car, right?"

"Feel free to lean forward and find out, but I really don't want or need to see that much of Scott if she's doing what I think she's doing."

Lea props her head against the window, the glass cool against her temple, staring out at the stars twinkling in the sky, and doing her best to try to ignore what could potentially be happening in the seat in front of her. Scott turns up the radio slightly, further fuelling her imagination.

"Should I say something?" Emerald suggests.

"Like what?" Raven's sarcasm oozes, "Would you mind not engaging in your intimate moments until I get out of the car? I hate to interrupt, but would it be possible to wait until I fall asleep

so I don't have to hear anything? What exactly is the appropriate thing to say in this situation?"

"Point taken, but you don't have to be so snide."

"I'm not snide. I'm irritated... and I find it offensive."

"Wait! Back the bus up. You find that offensive? I'm calling a big red bull pucky flag on that one!"

"I don't find THAT offensive. I find this particular timing of ... that... offensive."

"Thanks for that clarification. Well, Raven, if I shouldn't say anything, what should I do?"

"Pretend to sleep. Focus on the music and the stars."

"That'll work for Lea, but what about us?"

"What did that cop's eyes look like again?"

Emerald sighs. "They looked like the sky on the edges of a spring storm. Clear and blue, but tainted with the grey of roiling clouds, with a mysterious intensity that could be power, danger or could unleash a lightning bolt through you."

"All that from a glimpse in his eyes? Okay then."

Emerald stares out into the night sky. The radio station comes back from a block of commercials. Lea's eyes close. She knows this song, the soft piano introduction. This is the first song she and John ever danced to.

"So, Emerald... Tell me about John's eyes."

Raven can't resist the pull into the memory of being in John's room, frustrated that he would never dance with her in public, insisting on it since he was protected by the privacy behind closed doors, his mother not yet home from work, his father still asleep on the other side of his bedroom wall, John's choice of whatever song he wanted. He puts in a Journey cd, grabs the remote for his stereo, and goes right to it.

Just behind the door he steps up to her, arms open. She looks up at him and wraps her hands behind his neck. He reaches around behind her and holds her close to him. She rests her head *against his shoulder and closes her eyes as they sway back and forth, breathing in the scent of him, feeling the warmth of his touch surrounding her, never wanting the song or the moment to end.*

"John's eyes? John's eyes aren't the glimpse and catch kind." *Emerald's voice dissolves into a breathy wisp of a dream as she continues,* "His eyes are kind and trusting, innocent and tender. They make me think of cocoa on a cold winter's night... sweet, warm and welcoming. They melt you from the inside, making you feel safe, and there's a spark of a smile every time he looks at me."

"Anything else?" *Raven teeters on the edge of honest curiosity and condescension.*

"Love. If I stare into his eyes too long, I get butterflies in my stomach and giddy tingles all over."

"Lea? Lea?" Scott tries to get Lea's attention.

"What was Scott saying?" *Emerald snaps out of her fantasy.*

"How would I know? I was listening to your drunken babble about John's potable brown eyes."

"Huh?" Lea awakens from her inner repartee. "I'm sorry. What were you saying?"

Scott repeats himself, "I was just asking if you enjoyed yourself tonight."

"Oh, yeah, it was fine." Lea politely answers, wanting to zone back out instead.

"I know it got off to a rough start." Scott's voice wavers slightly.

"Dude! I get that you're trying to keep up polite conversation here, but can you please just let me go back to ignoring you two?" *Raven yearns to tell him what she really thinks of this predicament.*

"You could say that, but it's been a rough month just trying to get here." Lea responds diplomatically.

"It got better though right?" He shifts slightly in his seat.

"Let it go already. You're distracted enough from your driving without trying to uphold a conversation with me." Raven is growing more and more perturbed.

"Yeah, just a little tiring. It's been a long day." Lea yawns, hoping he'll drop the conversation and let her stare out into the vastness of space again.

"Pretty stars, pretty stars, pretty stars..." Emerald chants, covering her ears to keep from hearing any unwanted noises, and staring up and out, trying to imagine either herself floating amongst the stars or if John looks at the stars and thinks of Lea, anything other than being in this car right now.

Scott thankfully gives up the attempt at conversation. Lea shifts her head back against the glass. An indeterminable sound escapes the forward space.

"Raven, what was that?"

"Do you want the truth or do you want me to lie?"

"Lie."

"Well then, it was most likely just the sound of something shifting across the leather."

"If that's the lie, what the heck is the truth?"

"Well, in my best guesstimation..."Raven begins.

Emerald interrupts, "Never mind. I don't want to know. Couldn't you come up with something better for the lie?"

"Sure I could, but you didn't say you wanted unbelievable fiction."

"Give me the unbelievable fiction!"

"In that case, it was a glitch in the time portal from when we were stopped by the aliens and Scott and Rachel were taken aboard, studied, probed, and returned to the instantaneous moment that they were taken, but the advanced programming stuttered and didn't time it just right, leaving a small hiccup of

space where the replacing of them in the car left a millisecond of outbreak sound and that's what we heard, an alien glitch."

Emerald smiles, "Thank you, Raven. I like that version much better."

Lea looks for landmarks among the fields to try to determine where they are.

"Hey Raven, how much farther do you think it is?"

"I'd say 'bout halfway at best."

Slightly less nervous due to her subliminal fabrications, Lea addresses Scott, "Do you mind if I lay down back here?"

Scott catches his breath, "What was that?"

Lea repeats herself, "I was wondering if it would be okay if I were to lie down and maybe take a nap?"

"That's fine. I'll wake you when we get to your place."

"I appreciate that." Lea falls over and feigns sleep for the remainder of the drive.

"You know, Raven, why don't I just sleep? Everything gets tuned out when I sleep."

"Because I talk in my sleep," Raven replies, "but I can't control what I say. Do you trust what might come out of my mouth under these conditions? I don't. Besides, I thought about that already and, if I could have relaxed enough, I probably would have been out before now."

Scott lets out a heavy sigh.

"Raven, do you think it's possible that nothing's really going on? That maybe she's just sleeping? That Scott's shifting and whatnot is maybe him merely trying not to fall asleep himself?"

"Anything's possible. If it makes you feel better to believe that, Emerald, then fine. Do what you gotta do, but I'm not the eternal optimist that you are. I don't think the best of people. More

often than not, I think the worst of humanity in general. That's why I'm not as shocked as you are by the all the disappointing, horrible things people can do to each other."

"I know. I wish you didn't have to think that way all the time."

"If I don't, then who will? It's because I acknowledge and expect the worst from everything and everyone that you don't have to. It's who we are. Have I complained about it?"

"No."

"Okay then. Can you still see the stars?"

"Yes."

"Think they'll be this nice for graduation?"

"Hope so, a nice clear, rain free night."

"Think there's any chance KewpieMom will let us stay out all night?"

"That would be so nice, and she did allow Ginger and Vikki."

"Think you can come up with a plan for that? I, of course, will poke holes all through it because that's what I do, but it's bound to be better than tonight."

"Of course it will. John will be home!"

Lea grins at the idea as it waltzes through her mind.

Emerald continues, "As long as John's parents are going to be home, maybe I can go over there and watch movies all night."

"Can you remember the last time I made it through more than one movie with him without crashing?"

"Not the point."

"So what then is your point?"

"My point is he wouldn't have to wake me up to take me home."

"Aren't you forgetting something, or someone, dear Emerald?"

"Obviously I am or you wouldn't be asking. What did I

miss?"

"Allie."

"What about Allie?"

"Didn't she say that she is going to talk to her mother about staying out late with me?"

Emerald bites her lip, concentrating. "Okay, we'll all go do something together, and then after we take Allie home, I'll go back to John's with him."

"And what, pray tell, will we all be doing together? It's not like there's a whole lot of late night options in such a small town."

"I don't know. Do I have to have all the details right now? I have a couple weeks to iron things out. There's always the diner."

Lea's eyes pop open, and she shuts them quickly. She can't tell at first who it is, but somebody's breathing is getting quick and labored. She fills in the blanks when it's followed by a near silent, "Shhh" ... from Scott.

"So do you still think I was wrong in my assumptions?" Raven flicks her words at Emerald like carnival darts flying towards their balloon targets. Pop!

"Do you have to be so smug and cocky when you're right?" Emerald is growing noticeably agitated at the dissipation of her more polite theory.

"I'm not cocky. As for being smug, yes, yes I do."

"But you're not cocky?"

"Nope."

"How do you get that?"

"Easy. Cocky is when you're arrogant without a reason to be. I have a reason. I'm right, so I can't be considered cocky."

"Hey, was that a turn?"

"Yep. Got another wrench to toss at you."

"What now?"

"While you're working on ironing out your details, you might want to think about how exactly you think you're going to *get permission to spend the night with John without Dad thinking that you're going to be doing the same thing that was just going on or worse. I grant that you might be able to get around KewpieMom, but Dad is a completely different story."*

"Exactly! I get Mom to say yes, and she can deal with Dad. Perfect idea. Another turn. Think it's safe to sit up yet?

"That isn't exactly what I was saying, and I'd give it one more turn."

Lea stirs in the seat, but doesn't get up. One more turn and Lea shifts and sits up halfway, looking around as if she's trying to get her bearings. Realizing how close they are, she sits up the rest of the way.

At long last, Scott pulls onto Lea's road. She gathers her stuff efficiently, but without the frenzy that's writhing just beneath her skin. Her hand rests on the door eagerly awaiting the moment she can escape.

"Stop the car, put it in park, let me out, let me out, let me out...." Emerald is posed to burst out of the door like an Olympic sprinter exploding off the blocks, the click of the gear shift being the start gun.

"Calm down already! We're home. We got through this by pretending total cluelessness. If you go leaping out of a moving car, it's going to nullify all of that and then everyone is going to feel awkward." Raven chastises Emerald. *"Now deep slow breaths. In and out."*

Emerald does her best to follow Raven's instructions. The whole point is deliberate oblivion, maintain that air, maintain that façade, just a little but longer.

The car rolls to a stop in Lea's driveway next to Carl's van.

"I wonder how long they've been here." Emerald changes her focus, further helping her renewed composure.

Lea moves deliberately when Scott puts the car in

park, forcing herself to be slower than she wants to be. She thanks him again as she steps out.

"Anytime," Scott answers. Lea shuts the door and heads towards the house. Scott waits for the front door to open before he pulls away. Lea turns and waves good bye.

KewpieMom greets Lea as she comes through the door. "I'm so glad you're home. You okay? What happened?"

"I'm fine. What's wrong with you?" Her mother's excessive concern perplexes Lea.

"I heard you guys were stopped and drug searched," Mom says.

"Who told you that?" Lea glares over at Allie and Carl.

Allie fesses up, "We weren't sure if that was you or not until we got back here and you hadn't gotten dropped off yet."

"Alright, I can follow that, but where does the drug search come in?"

"Well, there was a cop parked behind you, and it looked like he was going through the trunk looking for something."

Lea shakes her head from side to side. Turning back to her mother, she tries to set the record straight. "It wasn't a drug search. Dave's car broke down shortly after we left. His clutch went out, which is located in the trunk of his car." Lea shoots Allie a look as she continues the tale, "Officer Friendly was just trying to help figure out what was wrong. Scott stopped and gave me a ride back."

"What about Dave? Where's he?" Carl finally spoke up.

"His parents were already on their way down, so he stayed with the officer to wait for them."

"Well, that's a relief," Lea's mom let out a sigh. "Allie told me about what happened with the seating. How was the ride home?"

"Don't ask. I don't want to talk about it, and it's nothing personal, Carl, but Mom may I take the car? I've had enough tonight of riding with other people."

"Sure, keys are by the door. Be careful." Mom motions to a table next to the front door.

Lea gives her mother a hug and whispers in her ear, "I promise I will be." She pulls back and adds, "I don't know how late I'll be."

"As long as you get back before you father wakes up, you should be fine."

Lea turns to Allie. "Why don't you two go ahead and get to the diner. Let everyone know we didn't bail on them? I'm just going to grab and bag my clothes. I can change when we get to the party."

"See you in a few..." Carl opens the door for Allie and escorts her to his van.

Lea drops off her prom favors and flowers on the kitchen table, grabs what she needs and gives her mother another hug and kiss goodbye, "Love you. I know you don't like to sleep when your children are out, but you look wiped. Try to get some rest. I'll be careful."

"Love you, too. I'll see you in the morning." Lea's mother heads to bed as Lea walks out the door.

Rose continues her narrations. As Lea drives away, her mother sees the carnations wilting on the table. She can't leave them there to wither and die prematurely and picks them up, cuts the ends and places them in a vase. She leaves the vase on the table and picks up Lea's picture frame.

"That's cute. What a clever idea." Mom says to herself.

She stands it next to the flowers and continues off to bed.

~ *Dine In or Carry Out* ~

Lea enjoys the solitude of her drive to the diner. Finally some peace and quiet eases her frazzling nerves, nothing and nobody to detrimentally inspire her imagination with repugnant triggers, just her, the rumbling lullaby of the tires rolling over the payment, and the radio. Always she has the music, and, apparently, a perfectly possessed car. She pushes the button to seek a new station. The numbers rush through sequence, passing over strong and known stations, to settle on deeper, darker, dulcet melodies.

Emerald dances along, not in the carefree prancing way like she does with Thistle. Her body rolls and twists and shifts beneath her robes, letting the music pulse through her, banishing her stress, and filling her with a tranquil repose. Her movements aren't the graceful balance of a ballerina, but then again, she doesn't have a ballerina's build anyway. She flows more like a green veil seductively undulating in a light breeze. Raven leans back letting the moon shine brightly down upon her and smiles as the dark techno harmonies reenergize both her companion and herself.

Lea could have made it to the diner in less than fifteen minutes, but she chose not to push it and took closer to twenty before she pulled into the parking lot. She spies Carl's van, Jason's car and an ominous line of both state and county patrol cruisers.

"You've got to be kidding me? I'm being stalked by cops!" *Raven shakes her head in disbelief.*

"Policeman's ball at The Hickville Diner, but it's almost midnight. Maybe we'll get to see them all turn into pumpkins." *Emerald's humor tickles her dark compadre.*

"Careful. Sounds like I'm rubbing off on you."

"Maybe a little, but is that really a bad thing?"

"As long as we don't end up switching roles. Being that peppy all the time would make me nauseous." *Emerald jokes back as Lea finds a space next to Jason's car and pulls in.*

The eatery is a small mom and pop spot, with good food and reasonable prices. It's been losing popularity with more and more big corporate choices moving into the growing city just outside of her small town. Lea likes the personality of the joint, and it's staffed by polite locals that always seem to have a smile for everyone. They stay open late on Friday and Saturday nights, but are completely closed Sundays.

The officers are all lined down the medium sized bar towards the back, just in front of the kitchen pass through, with the overflow sitting at the two tables closest to the kitchen door. The radios on their heavily clad batman belts still on, volume lowered. A few of them turn and look quickly as Lea walks in, their heightened observational awareness an understandable side effect of their line of work. They turn back to their meals.

Lea scans the quaint room. County music is piped

softly through speakers in the ceiling, matching the rural, down-home, family friendly, barn themed accessories that adorn the walls and tables. Varied brown and black tiles randomly cover the floor with no sense of pattern and wood accents throughout the room lend a warm and homey feel to the establishment.

It's busier than she expected with people filling almost three quarters of the quaint tables. A few of them are also in formal attire, although Lea doesn't recognize anyone. Most of them are in more casual threads. The majority of the patronage tonight is from the younger crowd with a handful of booths seating middle age men and women either on lunch or shift change from their factory jobs.

Lea locates her posse at a large top booth furthest from the officer encamped bar in the corner that backs up to the foyer entrance. Allie waves her over and scoots to make room at the crowded table. Jason is still in his lightly soiled work coveralls. He's stands and lets Lea sit next to her best friend.

"How was work tonight?" Lea asks as she scoots in to give him space to sit back down.

Jason unzips the top of his coveralls and ties them around his waist, revealing a much cleaner black t-shirt underneath. "Kinda slow. Lost track of time and rushed through closing. I didn't bother changing 'cause I thought I was going miss to meeting you guys. Should've known I wouldn't be the last one here." He lightly elbows Lea as he sits down next to her. He turns his head and whispers in her ear. "Truthfully, I think I feel asleep there for a little bit."

Lea snickers at their private exchange and pokes him back in his ribs. "Didn't Carl and Allie fill you in?"

"She said you guys were in that car we all passed that had gotten pulled over," Gail answers from the opposite side of the table. Lea takes notice of Rook sitting on the other opening, trying not to make eye contact with her, but also slightly relieved that Lea's mood seems to have improved.

Lea maps who all is here, and missing, as she circles the table with her eyes before resting a look of frustration on her best friend. On the other side of Gail is DiAna, then Nick, Carl and lastly Allie.

"What is this girl trying to do to me?" Raven glares at Allie.

"Where are Mike and Michelle? Brian and Lauren aren't here either." Emerald is almost equally annoyed for completely different reasons.

"That's not what I said!" Allie jumps to her own defense. "I said it was the car on the side of the road where the police car was. I did NOT say you guys got pulled over."

"So no drug search in this version?" Lea clarifies with her defensive friend.

A waitress steps next to the table, halting the conversation. She's wearing an orange and brown plaid apron over her yellow and brown uniform dress, order pad and pen in hand. "Can I get you anything, Dear?"

"A soda would be great." Lea answers and looks around the table to see if anyone else still needs to order.

"Anything to eat?" the pleasantly average looking, thirty-something waitress asks.

"No, thank you. Just a drink, please." Lea answers politely and focuses back on the members of the group as their waitress leaves. "Where's everyone else? Mike... Michelle... Brian?"

"Mike and Michelle said they wouldn't be coming. Pretty sure they're breaking up tonight," Gail offers. "Have no idea what the deal is with Brian."

Lea turns to Allie. "I forgot. Did you remember to

remind him to meet us here?"

"Oh crap. No. But I didn't see them when we walked out either." Allie answers.

"This makes things a smidgen complicated." Raven starts *pacing, trying to come up with a new plan.*

"Maybe Jason knows where the house is?" Emerald *suggests.*

The waitress returns with Lea's drink and places it in front of her.

"Thanks," Lea acknowledges her and takes a sip.

"Will there be anything else?" The waitress addresses the entire table.

Everyone nods negatively. "That's it for now. Thank you." Lea speaks for the group and then tilts her head to shield her face as she quietly asks Jason, "By some miracle, do you know where Shane lives?"

"Who?" Jason whispers back.

"Shane Pence."

"No, why?"

"He's supposed to be having the after prom party, but Brian's the only one that knows where he lives."

"Oh."

Allie interrupts them, "Let me out. I have an idea."

Startled, Jason and Lea step up as Allie works her way around the table's bench, then scurries over to the diner's pay phone. They sit back down curious to what the quirky youngster is scheming.

Rook launches a new conversation, "So Nick, do you mind if I ask how you became blind? You said something earlier that made me think you used to be able to see. Have you been blind long? Did something happen?"

DiAna flops her head backwards and rolls it slowly back up, shooting Rook an 'I can't believe you just asked that' scowl, aware of what's coming.

Nick is unbothered and flippant as he answers, his tone entwined with a hint of expectation, like he's been waiting all night for the subject to come up. "You're right. I wasn't always blind. In fact, I lost my sight just a few years ago."

"What happened?" Rook's curiosity encourages Nick to continue.

"I missed," Nick replies. DiAna lets her face fall into her palm.

"What?" Gail asks completely confused by Nick's answer.

"I was trying to kill myself, so I took a gun and I was gonna blow my brains out, but I aimed wrong, and just blew out my eyes instead. I missed." Nick clarifies with a matter of fact nonchalance like he's telling us all how to boil an egg.

The entire table falls silent, mouths dropping open in utter disbelief. The stillness in the air so complete that Lea can hear the hushed clicks and reports from the police radios on the other side of the room.

Crickets chirp around Emerald and Raven, accentuating the uncomfortable lack of sound. "Raven! Say something!" Emerald pleads.

"What the hell do you expect me to say to that? I don't have some filing cabinet I can sift through for how to respond to completely inappropriate and awkward situations!" Raven retorts dumbfounded by the revelation.

"Well, why not? You've got something to say any other time!"

"Attempted suicide is a new one for me! I'll see what I can work up in case we run across another moment like this!" Raven snaps.

Nick reaches out, seeking his glass, and pulls it

towards him, taking a drink. His cheeks lifted, giving the air that he's laughing at all of us behind the dark black sunglasses that he's worn all night.

Jason breaks the dead calm, his stomach bouncing with secret soundless chuckles, "Are you serious or are you messing with us?"

"Both," Nick confesses. "Yes, that's really how it happened, but I really love hearing the reaction when I tell people, or more to the point, NOT hearing it. I can take off my glasses and show you if you want me to prove it."

"That won't be necessary," DiAna puts a stop to the potential show and tell, dashing Rook's morbid eagerness before he can pounce on the offer.

Rook begins to ask something else, but Gail punches him in the thigh under the table, and he reconsiders the attempt.

"Before this gets out of hand, let me skim through the highlights. Obviously, I was having some pretty severe depression issues. Thought everything about life sucked, issues with my parents, very few friends, just got dumped by a girl, I was a total screw up, getting into trouble. Thought everyone would be better off without me and life wasn't worth living. Bang!"

"You don't seem that messed up now, maybe a dark and twisted sense of humor, but..." Lea begins.

"I'm not. For whatever reason, I missed. And you'd think that would be really hard to do that close, but I did, and I'm still here. It changed my view on life." Nick laughs at his play on words, "In LOTS of ways! I can't seem to see things the same way I used to." Lea and Jason are the first two to start laughing with Nick at the bad joke.

The whole table is cracking up when Allie bounces back next to Jason. "What'd I miss?"

"Don't ask!" Lea answers.

"Okay?" Allie's still not sure exactly what's going on. Everyone starts laughing harder.

"I'll tell ya later," Lea reassures her.

Jason begins to stand so Allie can have her spot back. "Nah, just scoot over." Lea slides next to Carl and Allie plops on the end next to Jason. Carl has moved beyond the constant slights from her and ignores the latest strategic move to further her position of noninterest.

"Speaking of not asking…" Nick prompts, making his previous audience wonder where he can be leading this time. "What's the story behind the drug search?"

"Ugh!" Lea exhales, preferring not to have to rehash it all.

"Come on," Nick urges. "I shared. Your turn. Besides that's basic Mary Jane etiquette. Puff, puff, pass to the left."

"One, I'm not even going to ask how you would know that, and, two, I'm to your right." Lea stalls.

"If you go to the left enough times, it'll come back around to you, and I told you that I used to be a screw up. I know lots of things. Some of which are much more interesting when your hands are acting as your eyes." DiAna blushes as Nick wiggles his fingers I the air and raises his eyebrows above his glasses and smiles at his innuendo.

Carl chokes on his drink.

Lea leans away, reflexively trying to protect herself from a repeat explosion, not realizing she's all but put herself in Jason's lap.

"Hel-lo!" Jason proclaims, enjoying the twist the conversation has taken and the proximity of her new position. Lea looks up over her left shoulder at Jason, feeling his chest against her back and fully absorbing how they must look.

DiAna whispers in Nick's ear, and he starts laughing loudly.

Lea's face flushes with heat, and her cheeks blush a bright red, clashing with her peach dress. "Oh my God! I am so sorry." She leans back up to her place next to Carl, who is still coughing, trying to clear his drink, and laughing at the same time.

"Didn't bother me any," Jason taunts.

Lea looks to Allie for a little help to ease her humiliation, but finds Allie's glare cool in return.

"What's that about?" Raven grumbles.

"What's what about?" Emerald looks around trying to figure out what Rave's referring to.

"That snarky look from Allie." Raven explains.

"Maybe she's getting tired." Emerald suggests.

"Maybe…" Raven keeps watching Allie to further examine her glare and see if it changes.

"So shall we get back to your drug search?" Nick asks of Lea. "I could go on about the benefits of being blind if you prefer."

"No, no, no. I'll explain," Lea volunteers to keep the conversation from the landslide rush downward that it could take otherwise.

"If you insist," Nick smiles, leans back, lifts his arm and wraps it around DiAna's shoulders.

"First of all, it WASN'T a drug search, so I think you'll find it disappointing, but that's what Allie told my MOTHER" Lea drags out the word mother as she relates the snag in her night, "when she got to my house before I did. The clutch broke. The cop was trying to help, and I ended up getting a ride with someone else that recognized Dave's car. See, not that interesting."

"Then why do I get the feeling there's something

you're leaving out?" Nick presses further.

"Maybe there is, maybe there isn't. Either way, that's all I'm saying about it." Lea parries back.

"Dave didn't try something, did he?" Gail sputters out, missing the intention of the verbal banter.

Lea's startled by the thought and shudders, "Ew! No! Nothing like that."

"Lea's not the one he's hoping to…" Allie trails off and ceases her comment when Lea clears her throat and flails daggers at her visually.

Raven throws her arms up in the air. "So many great things about this girl, but the brain-mouth filter is NOT one of them."

"I'd gotten that totally out of my mind too." Emerald adds.

"Happy visuals return," Raven's voice drips with distain as an image appears over them, a projected movie of Dave making out with Ginger.

"I think I'm going to be sick." Emerald covers her mouth with her hand and bends over, and the film fades to black.

Raven brings her a glass of water. "It's gone."

Emerald appeals to her, "Don't let them pounce on Allie's comment. Make them change the subject, please."

Lea leans forward, keeping her voice from carrying through the restaurant. "Speaking of police, am I the only one that noticed the seven to ten cop cars outside?"

"They were pulling in right as I got here." Jason volunteers. Rook, Gail, and DiAna all look over, apparently unaware since the group would have filed in behind them.

"Dunkin' Doughnuts must be closed," Nick bellows.

"Oh shit! HIDE!" Raven screams. She and Emerald dive behind Raven's walls.

Seven of the eight bodies go diving or sliding below the table line. Jason, Allie, and Gail join Lea beneath the table seeking an imaginary contact lens that nobody's lost. Carl, Rook, and DiAna take advantage of the extra space and lie across the bench, leaving Nick as the sole occupant of the large top.

Lea dares to look in the direction of the officer occupied bar. About half of the boys in blue have taken note of the comment and turned to face the offender.

"We are so screwed. They are going to wait for us and give all of us tickets." Raven points to the officers, keeping her voice hushed.

Emerald stands up. "Why are we hiding? Nobody can see us?" She plops on Raven's settee. "They are officers of the law. They have better things to do than silliness like that."

Most of the officers now watching their table begin chuckling at the sight of a single, tux-clad, young man in sunglasses sitting at the large table by himself, colorful bodies huddled beneath it. They turn back to their meals and their conversations.

Jason has also peered over at the lawmen. "I think it's clear now, but we should probably get outta here."

"But where are we gonna go?" DiAna asks from the bench.

"My house!" Allie announces. Everyone looks at her as she continues, "I went to call my mom since Brian bailed on us. She said we could watch movies there if we wanted. She's whipping up some munchies for us now. We just can't get super loud cause Dad's sleeping."

"Love this girl!" Emerald applauds.

"Freaking awesome! We're outta here." Raven climbs out and takes her place next to Emerald.

"Perfect! Let's get the check," Lea states retreating back up to her seat.

As the group of teens recomposes themselves around

the table, Jason waves down their waitress. "Could we get the check, please?"

She nods her head back towards the assembly of uniforms, "It's already been taken care of."

The teens look over to see two of the officers raise their drinks in a toast, still laughing.

Their waitress continues through a wide smile, "They said you could probably use the extra money to get those dresses cleaned after crawling on the floor." She turns away with a bounce and leaves the now pink cheeked, giggling group to try and disperse without any further incident.

"I don't know where you live, Allie," Rook states as he stands, extending his hand to help Gail and DiAna out as well.

"Why don't you guys go ahead and follow Carl and Allie there? I'll take care of the tip." Lea offers, getting out of the way for Carl to leave.

Carl tosses out a couple dollars on the table to add as he stands. He sweeps his hand in a chivalrous gesture giving Allie the lead. Jason stays behind with Lea, throwing in on the tip as well.

"Do you mind if I ride over with you? We can swing back by here and pick up my car on the way home." He asks.

She grabs up Carl and Jason's money, adds hers to it, and leaves it in a neat stack in the middle of the table. "That's fine," Lea answers, looking past him at the generous officers.

"You didn't just hang back to take care of the tip, did you?" He follows her stare.

"No," she drops her eyes and looks back up at Jason.

"I need to get out of these things," he pulls on the tied sleeves of his coveralls. "I'll throw them in my car and meet you outside." Jason smiles before leaving

Lea hollers lightly to him, "My car's right next to yours."

"I know. I saw ya when ya pulled in." Jason pushes on the door and walks out.

Lea takes in a deep breath and heads over to the bar of officers.

"Emerald, what are you doing?" Raven grabs ahold of the green robes as Emerald walks towards her own bench.

"Being polite," Emerald swats at her hands.

"You don't have to do this. Stop."

"Should and have to aren't always the same thing."

"Fine," Raven releases her grip, "but I don't want to hear about their eyes this time."

Lea stops behind the two that toasted them, clears her throat, suddenly very nervous and feeling very parched, her head down sheepishly. "Excuse me."

They both turn around, and the rest of the group takes notice.

Lea looks up, but can't make eye contact. "I wanted to apologize for the gentleman's comment and say thank you for picking up our tab."

The officer on her right, an older gentleman with slightly greying hair at his temples and shallow wrinkles around his eyes when he smiles, wipes his mouth with his napkin. In a gravelly voice, he replies, "You're welcome. No need to apologize. The sight of him sitting there all alone and you all melting under the table trying to hide was the best laugh we've had in a while."

Lea nods shyly and steps back to leave.

The other officer, a larger, younger, burly man, the size of a professional football player with arms like small tree limbs, adds, "Miss, we're about done here, and we're going to be out there watching, so I hope you all plan on staying out of trouble and not driving if you shouldn't be," obviously being serious in his warning but keeping a smile in his voice.

Lea pauses to answer him. "Not a problem, Sir. We're not that group. Just hanging out and watching movies. We'll be good." She flashes them a smile and heads for the door.

"Suck up!" Raven huffs at Emerald.

"Maybe, but they can obviously see what I'm driving if they want to, and you're paranoid. So if I need to suck up a little to make sure I don't get pulled over, so be it." Emerald retorts with smug accomplishment.

~ Flicks and Fantasies ~

Jason's leaning against Lea's driver's door as she approaches.

"I hope he doesn't think I'm going to let him drive. Why do guys always think they HAVE to drive everywhere?" Raven complains.

"You don't seem to mind when John drives everywhere." Emerald counters.

"That's different. We're always in John's car. This isn't his car, and Jason isn't John!" Raven grows more agitated.

"Be nice. We like Jason. He's a good guy. He's just trying to be gentleman." Emerald attempts to keep Raven calm.

Lea reaches the car, and Jason opens the driver's door, "Your chariot, M'lady," bowing and swooping his arm widely.

"Thanks," Lea snickers at his theatrical display.

"All that fuss for nothing," Emerald laughs.

"Blah, Blah, Blah. Shut up." Raven grumbles and crosses her arms.

Lea steps in and Jason closes her door before circling

around to jump in the passenger's side. Lea pulls out and starts on the short trip to Allie's house.

"So what'd ya end up sayin' to 'em? And what is this crap you're listening to?" Jason asks.

"I apologized for the comment, thanked them for paying, and I don't know. They weren't playing that on the way in."

Jason plays with the radio, looking for something more agreeable to his ear. "They say anything interesting?" He gives up and settles on the local top forty station.

"Not really, but I wouldn't speed on your way home later."

"Good ta know. So how did your night really go?"

"Don't ask. I think this has been the best part so far."

"Come on. It couldn't have been that bad."

Lea chuckles sarcastically to herself, then fills him in on the events leading up to when she arrived at the diner. She swears him to secrecy and includes the auditory voyeurism in the Cadi.

"Wow. Really?" Jason is stunned. "I wouldn't have thought Rachel was that daring."

"Guess so."

"And they didn't care that you were there?"

"They think I was asleep... And they're going to continue to think I was asleep, right? I'm not saying anything to anyone about that except you, so I'll know if it gets around."

"I won't say a word. That stays between you and me."

Rook is parked behind Carl's van as Lea pulls into Allie's drive. She takes the spot behind Allie's mother's car, filling up the small inclined cement pad in front of their attached garage.

"Not a word," Lea reiterates to Jason as they step out of the car. She grabs her bag of clothes from the back and heads in. Jason knocks softly and opens the door for her.

Allie is ready to greet them, having already changed from her formal dress to comfy pajamas. She leads them through the living room, past the kitchen, to the family room at the back of the house. "Mom headed to bed already, but the backroom is all ours. There's food in the kitchen... chips and veggies and dip, cheese and crackers, and some cut up lunchmeat sandwiches, so help yourself. Soda's in the garage frig." Addressing them directly she adds, "I know what Lea likes to drink. What can I get for you, Jason?"

"Surprise me," he grins.

Allie steps out the door, leaving them to get comfortable in the modest, but heavily furnished, family room. There is a small couch in each of the far back corners. Nick and Carl have claimed the dark almond sofa on the right. DiAna is on the floor in-between Nick's legs. Rook and Gail are in the center of the room on the floor lying across the nature print area rug, propping themselves up with the throw pillows off the sofas. This leaves the deep, muted blue sofa on the left and a matching oversized cushy chair against the garage wall in front of Carl open for them to choose from. Jason heads over to the sofa, and Lea takes claim to the chair, flopping into it sideways and letting her legs drape over the arm and kicking off her shoes. The oversized TV sits diagonally into the room facing Nick and Carl directly.

Allie returns with drinks for everyone, circling the room as she hands them out. "So did y'all decide on a movie yet?" she inquires of nobody in particular.

"No foreign films with subtitles," Nick offers up as Allie places his can against his hand. "I have real trouble following those."

"No romantic chic flicks!" Carl tosses out. Rook agrees.

"Nothing scary," Lea voices her objections. "I've had enough horror for tonight."

Jason chuckles to himself, "I'd pick a different genre to describe parts of it, but action or comedy it is!"

Lea tilts her head backwards and to the side to scowl at him, but Jason just ignores it, "You know if you're upside down when you frown it just looks like you're smiling."

Lea juts her tongue out at him.

"Now, now. You don't want me telling John you were making me offers," he needles her.

Allie pulls out three movies. "'Raiders', 'Ferris', or 'Legend'?"

'Ferris Bueller' wins, and she puts it in. Everyone gets comfy and Allie sits next to Jason on the blue couch. Lea snuggles into her chair and drifts off to sleep. She opens her eyes briefly when she hears the guys ogling the sports car.

"Men have no clue what a pain it is to have to get in and out of those things, do they?" Emerald whines lightly.

"They don't care," Raven corrects. "If they were the ones wearing heels, they'd all want to drive taller vehicles."

"And how do they expect us to always look like a supermodel if it's a convertible and our hair is blowing all over and whipping in our face?"

"Again…. They don't care."

DiAna joins in their dialogue, "I'd drive a car like that."

Lea mumbles, "And you'd arrive everywhere looking like a blonde Bride of Frankenstein. A car like that takes 'wind-blown' to a whole different level. That's why in older movies you always see the women wearing scarves tied around their heads. " She yawns and drifts off to sleep again.

Lea floats into a continuation of her dream of John being with her tonight. She's back on the dance floor with him, holding each other close, oblivious to their surroundings. Everyone else is just blurs of grey shadow. They sway and move and the song changes, "Danke schoen, Darlin', danke schoen...."

"This isn't right," Raven lifts her out of her slumber.

Lea takes a swig of her drink and twists and wiggles in her chair to the movie. Allie throws a pillow at her.

"Thanks. I could use this." Lea stuffs it behind her head and keeps wriggling to the music. She readjusts herself, sliding smoothly into another slumber.

This time her mind meanders to a darkened gym, a spot light showering a beam of white down upon her. She's in the middle of a mat, but can't see anything beyond the edges of the illuminated circle. She feels a sharp pain in her back, a punch. The offender spins around in front of her. Although covered from head to toe in black and wearing a mask, Lea recognizes the figure. She'd know those blue eyes and cheek bones anywhere.

"What was that for?" Lea protests.

"After all that work I did to make you look good, you had to go and mess it all up," ninja Ginger swoops in and punches her in the face.

Lea swings and misses. Ginger whips around kicking her in the ribs before bouncing out of range again. She continues in this manner over and over, dash in, strike, then retreat out of range.

Lea whimpers in her sleep and rolls in her chair. Allie grabs a throw blanket and covers her friend, silencing her utterances.

Lea wipes the blood from her nose. She looks down at her dress. Taking in a deep breath and closing her eyes, she looks down again, but now she's wearing loose, flowing black pants, and her red school tee, a black panther leaping forward on the front, the phrase 'Nothing Behind You Matters' on the back.

Ginger comes flying in from the darkness, but this time Lea dodges the attack and grabs her flaxen locks, yanking her down to the ground. Ginger falls flat on her back but bounces back up and leaps away. Her eyes shine from just beyond the circle of light.

"All this over messed up make up?" Lea calls into the darkness.

"No. All this over every little thing you've ever done to annoy me," Ginger spits back.

"Like what? By all means share this list with me..." Lea spins looking for Ginger having lost her in the shadows.

"Let's start with being born," Ginger seethes as she leaps at Lea knocking her to the ground.

Before Lea can get back up, the blonde aggressor attacks again. Lea catches Ginger with her legs as Ginger lunges at her, flipping her over and crashing her into the floor. Lea rolls towards her sister, trying to take advantage of the moment, but falls victim to a kick to the face. She reverses course and rolls away, covering her swelling eye with her hand.

By sheer luck, Lea times her next defense perfectly as Ginger charges again. Lea throws out her arm stiffly, clotheslining her sister, who flips backwards in the air before landing face first on the ground like a bad game of red rover. Lea drops on Ginger's back, holding her down. Ginger kicks and tries to swing at Lea, flailing underneath her, struggling to free herself. Lea grabs Ginger's arms behind her, pinning her down.

"Enough!" Lea shouts down at Ginger, but gets struck

in the back of the head by an invisible force. When Lea looks back down, her hands are empty and Ginger is gone. She lifts her head to see her former captive standing four feet away, very free, and pacing like a cat ready to pounce.

"You just don't get it, do you?" Ginger taunts her. "As long as I am the golden child, you can never win. It doesn't matter what you say or what you do. It will never be good enough. I will always come out on top." With that, Ginger spins in a circle and kicks Lea in the head, hurling her into the darkness and ending her nightmare.

After the movie ends, Rook announces that he's getting tired and DiAna says she's needs to be getting home too. The four stand, taking a personal inventory that they have everything they came in with.

Gail motions towards Lea, "Should we wake her?"

"Don't worry about her. I'll take care of her. Sometimes she can be a bit difficult to get up." Allie waves them away from Lea.

The foursome heads towards the door with Carl close behind. He foregoes any attempt to get a good night kiss, knowing it would be a complete waste of time and effort. Allie walks them all to the door.

"Thanks for taking me tonight, Carl." She says as he steps out the door.

Carl turns, shocked by her sudden kindness. He grabs her fingers and gives her a kiss on the back of her hand. "You are very welcome. I hope you had a good time."

"I did." Allie pulls her hand away with more tenderness than she has shown all night. "Drive careful."

Carl walks towards his van, and Allie closes the door.

Jason slides up behind her, "Is Lea really that hard to wake up?"

Allie jumps at the sound of his voice, not realizing he

was there. "Yes and no."

"That clears everything up. What does that mean?"

"I don't think she's wants tons of people knowing."

"You can tell me. I'm learning all kinds of secrets tonight."

"Sometimes, when people think she's awake, she isn't."

"What!?!"

"She talks in her sleep."

"Okay. So? Lots of people do that."

"But do they also open their eyes, sit up and have complete conversations with no recollection of it other than a vague memory of it being a dream?"

"She does that?"

"Sometimes. You just have to make sure she's REALLY awake when you rouse her, and, with the night she's had, it's possible that might be an issue. I know she wouldn't want them knowing about that." Allie shifts her weight. "I'm not really tired if you wanted to stick around for another movie. Unless of course you need to be getting home...."

"I'm in no rush. She won't get in trouble if we let her sleep a little longer, will she?"

"'As long as she gets home before her dad wakes up.' That's what her mom said."

"Cool. We're good. What's next?"

Allie and Jason return to the family room, and she changes the movie. He plops back into the blue sofa. Allie grabs a large throw blanket before she sits down next to him, pulling her legs up under her and listing slightly towards him, testing his reception.

Jason gets the hint and runs with it, lifting his arm up on the back of the couch so she can lean up against him.

Allie snuggles in and pulls the blanket over both of them. Jason stretches his legs out and wraps his arm around her, smiling inappropriately.

The movie's barely begun before Allie and Jason start making out, kissing and snuggling. Lea rolls over to face them. Jason pauses, whispering to Allie, "Is she waking up?"

Allie halts and returns to a safer position just leaning against him, watching Lea closely. "I don't think so," she whispers back.

Lea rebounds from her battle with Ginger. She opens her eyes to find herself floating, all her wounds gone. The water is cool but not uncomfortably cold. She's outside and the sky is clear and full of stars. She lifts herself to look around, treading silently. She's never been here before. She's in a lake, there's a dock with a boat tied to it and a small grove of trees along the bank next to the beach. She can see a bonfire and hear voices and laughter, but she doesn't register any of them as familiar.

She leans her head back again, muting out the water lapping on the shore, the crackle of the embers, and the boisterous people gathered around it. She stares at the stars twinkling and shining, untethered, unbound, free and beautiful, but isolated, cold, and lonely. The tranquility of it all both soothing and inviting.

She takes a deep breath and drops below the surface. Through the water she hears music and swims towards it. Pomp and Circumstance hums in the distance. Lea slips out of the lake and into another dream.

She sees herself walking towards the temporary stage, dissolving into herself as she crosses and looks closely at her diploma as it's handed to her. She whips around to face her parents and John sitting together in the stands and gives them a thumbs up as she takes it and continues on.

John leans over to KewpieMom, "What was that about?"

"They spelled her name right," she answers.

Her thoughts time lapse to after the ceremonies are finished. She meets them in the hall, still in her red cap and gown and with Allie in tow. They all stand together as Allie takes the obligatory photos.

"So what's the plan? Mom said I could hang for a little while if you still wanted to?" Allie asks handing KewpieMom back the camera.

"I don't know what my time limit is tonight yet," Lea aims her statement at her mother.

"You've graduated. Curfew's gone. Have fun." Lea's dad shifts uncomfortably and looks at John as Lea's mother gives her free reign.

"Thanks," Lea hugs and kisses her mother.

She kisses her father's cheek and wraps her arms around him in a big hug. He can't help himself, softly telling her, "Be good," before giving her a tight squeeze and letting her go.

"Did you need to get a change of clothes from the house?" her mother asks.

"No, I'm good. I brought a set with me." Lea is completely prepared for tonight. "Allie, do you need clothes?"

"They're in my mom's car," she answers.

KewpieMom gives John a hug, "Drive careful."

"I will," he reassures her.

The trio heads out. Allie grabs her clothes and jumps in the backseat. She strips out of her dress and throws on capris pants and a tank top while John drives away from the school.

"So where are we going?" She asks as she stuffs her

dress and shoes in her bag.

"We could go to the diner," Lea offers up with no clue what the three could do so late at night.

"You aren't gonna believe this, but I... you... we were invited to a party." John announces.

"Are you kidding me? I haven't been invited to a party the entire time I went to school here and now that it's over, we're invited?" The irony catches Lea off guard.

"Whose party?" Allie asks.

"Tana's," John braces for Lea's reaction.

"Cool," Allie's excitement bursts before Lea can respond.

"Who told you?" Lea is apprehensive.

"Jackson and Ben stopped me when I first got there, and Tana came up while we were talking. Jackson said we should come by, and she agreed."

"You guys know who else is going to be there then," Lea is the only one seeing the issue.

"It'll be fine. We're here. Come on. Let's go!" Allie pushes from the back.

"Fine. Allie, hand me my bag. If you can change in route, so can I." Lea takes the bag as Allie passes it forward. She slides her pantyhose off under her miniskirt dress and puts them in the bag as she pulls out her shorts and shirt. She slides the shorts on under her skirt. She hands the bag back to Allie before pulling her dress over her head and sliding her shirt on. "Here," Lea hands the dress back, and Allie puts it in the bag for her.

John pretends he wasn't paying attention and continues to drive towards Tana's house. It's a larger two story in a nice neighborhood. Lea's still unsure as they walk towards the front door.

Tana meets them and welcomes them in. "Everyone's

out back by the pool. Follow me." The trio falls in line, Allie taking the lead and John holding Lea around the waist.

There are a couple dozen people out back, some older, most recently graduated, and a few up and coming seniors. Allie doesn't seem to notice or care that she's the youngest one there. Music is blaring at a semi-reasonable level, and several of them are carrying around wine coolers.

"Cooler is over there. If you plan on drinking..."

"No, thank you," Lea interrupts her.

"Well, there's soda in there too. Enjoy." Tana heads off to mingle through her guests.

Allie spies Ben sitting by himself and takes off to go chat with him. Lea grabs John's hand and finds a couple chairs over by the far corner of the pool.

"I need a drink. I'll be right back," John says and sets off in the direction of the cooler.

Lea is watching some of the girls dancing, not realizing her feet are shuffling to the beat, when Brandi spots her by herself. She bounces over and sits next to Lea. "Hey! Didn't expect to see you here."

"Jackson and Tana invited John."

"Cool. I wanted to tell you I liked your dress tonight. It looks cute on you."

"Thanks."

"You haven't seen Brent meandering around, have you?"

"No, but I'll let him know you're looking for him if I do."

Brandi flits off smiling. Lea looks around for John. He's just closed the cooler and is heading back, when she hears someone calling his name. She scans the shadows by the house where the voice came from. She sees a couple sharing a chair, she's sitting on his lap, but Lea can't make out who they are. John stops and walks over towards them. The girl gets up and moves off towards the dancing crowd. It's Jen, which means the guy must be Eric.

Eric stands and shakes John's hand, pulling him in and slapping him on the shoulder with his other hand. They head back over to Lea together.

"Hey. How's it going?" Eric asks her taking a swig of his wine cooler.

"Not bad. How've you been?" She returns the courtesy.

"Pretty good. I was just asking John if you guys would be interested in playing some euchre if we can wrangle up a fourth?"

"I'm in," Lea smiles.

"Why don't you two head in and grab the table in the kitchen before someone else does? I'll get us a fourth and meet you in there. There's usually a deck of cards in the top drawer closest to the table." Eric steps off towards the other side of the pool.

Lea checks for Allie, who's still talking with Ben and staying out of trouble, so she goes inside with John and gets the small glass top table ready.

Lea takes the seat with her back to the party. John's right across from her and can see everything. Lea's shuffling when Eric comes in and takes the seat on Lea's right. Lea looks up to see who's sitting to her left... Jackson Daniels.

"This ought to be interesting?" Jackson says.

Lea tenses.

"Why?" Eric asks.

"She and I are usually on the same team when we play. Don't think we've actually played against each other yet."

John smiles at Lea, knowing that's not what she was

thinking.

"I see," Eric looks up. "She any good?"

"Yeah, even when she's not stacking the deck," Jackson compliments her with a smile.

"Actually , maybe I should be asking John if she's any good." Eric grins and winks at Lea.

John smiles, but does not respond to Eric's comment.

Lea deals out the cards, and they each win a game. They're about halfway through the tie-breaking third game, when John looks up and gets a serious look on his face. "Jack," he murmurs and throws a glance behind Lea.

Lea catches the moment and is about to turn around with John minutely shifts his head side to side, warning her to keep her focus fixed on him. She knows exactly who's behind her.

"Oh shit!" Jackson mumbles softly.

"What?" Eric looks over to see Amanda glaring at Jackson.

"Don't ask," John cautions quietly.

Amanda is waving Jackson over to her. "Excuse me." He gets up from the table. The three left at the glass top can't help but overhear what ensues.

"You know, Jackson, it's bad enough that this is supposed to be our graduation party, and you've chosen to spend it playing cards with her," Amanda sneers as she says 'her,' "but now I'm hearing that you're the one that invited her. Is it true?"

Before Jackson can answer, Eric pipes up, "Looks like the game's over, and I could use a cigarette. You guys wanna come outside with me?"

"Hell yeah," John's already getting out of his seat.

Eric leads the way, and John keeps himself between Lea and the arguing couple.

"So what's all that about?" Eric asks Lea, lighting up a cigarette and nodding his head back inside.

"Long story. There's a history there." Lea answers.

"I can tell," Eric takes a long drag.

"It was really nice to see you, but I think we're going to head out," John puts his hand out to Eric.

"Good to see you too." Eric shakes John's hand. "Thanks for the game." He pats Lea on the shoulder. "You guys have fun tonight."

"Hoping to," Lea grins at Eric, knowing full well how he'll take it.

"Let's get what's her name and head out." John and Lea move toward where they last saw Allie talking to Ben.

Ben is standing, trying to wrestle Allie towards the pool edge. Allie struggles against him. "Hey John, grab her feet!" Ben calls out.

John grabs her feet, and Ben has gained control of her arms, hanging her like a hammock.

"Help me, Lea," Allie cries out to her friend.

"You're gonna need a towel. I'll get right on that!" Lea smiles and walks away to find Tana, who's joined everyone else watching the events unfold.

"1, 2, 3…" John and Ben count to each other as they swing Allie back and forth and release her flying and flailing into the pool.

"Tana, can we borrow a towel for Allie?" Lea asks, snickering at her sputtering pal as Allie tries to work her way to the edge. "We'll bring it back tomorrow. I promise."

"Sure," Tana laughs, handing Lea a thick beige towel from a stack on a nearby table. "Take this one."

Allie climbs out, soaked and dripping. Lea hands her the towel. "Thanks," Allie wipes off her face.

"Happy to help," Lea smiles widely. "You ready to

go?"

"Yeah, I wasn't expecting to need a spare set of clothes." Allie wraps the towel around herself and takes off her shirt to wring the water out. She puts it back on and repeats the process for her pants. "Here," Allie tries to hand the towel back to Lea.

"Tana said we can take it for John's car. We'll bring it back later," Lea informs her.

The trio heads out. Allie folds the towel and sets it between her and John's back seat. He drops Allie off at her house and heads back home.

Lea starts the conversation, "I can't believe she changed clothes in the back seat."

"You changed in the front. Nice bra."

"I was hoping you'd like it, and that's different."

"How?"

"We're engaged, and it's not like you haven't seen it all before."

"If you're implying that I was stealing looks at her, don't. I was too busy staring at your legs and the road."

"Ahhh…. You're so sweet."

"I'm happy with what I've got," John rubs his hand up and down her thigh.

"So you wouldn't want any more?"

"Depends on what you mean by more."

"You really need me to clarify that?" Lea runs her hand up the inside of John's thigh.

"Maybe, what exactly are you implying here?"

"That I want you to help me make tonight memorable."

"I'll have to see what I can do about that."

John pulls in his drive, and they quietly step inside, not sure who's awake or sleeping. The television is on in the front room, and the basement door is open. John goes downstairs to see who's up and inform them that they're home.

Lea heads into John's bedroom and tosses her bag on the far side of the bed. John steps in behind her and closes the door. "Dad's up. He said to keep it closed because Mom's already gone to bed and that way we won't wake her."

"Isn't that a convenient rule change?"

John leans over, pressing his lips to hers. She reaches her arms around his neck and returns his kiss. He pulls away and turns on his television.

"Any preferences?"

"Not really. I don't plan on paying much attention to it."

"So I've gathered, but just in case my dad does check in, it might help if something is on."

"In that case, pick anything you know I've already seen. That way I don't have to worry if I get asked what it's about."

John pops in 'The Princess Bride.' "I know you know this one forward and back."

"First movie we ever saw together." Lea lies back on his bed, feeling the water shift beneath her, reaching over the edge, and pulling her nightshirt from her bag. "That was a pretty interesting night too if I remember right."

"Be right back." He says as he grabs a pair of shorts and reaches for the door.

"Where you going?"

"To get us something to drink and not be too obvious since my dad's still awake."

Lea changes into her oversized night shirt and shoves everything back into her bag. She slides under John's covers and curls up on her side.

John returns with shorts on, jeans and sodas in hand. "Hmmm, there's a beautiful woman in my bed... whatever shall I do?" He drops his pants in the corner and closes the door behind him.

"Where?"

"Ha, ha." He sets the drinks on the nightstand and lies down next to Lea on the bed, above the covers.

"Are you really sure about this?" John kisses her neck and shoulder. "We don't have to. I can wait."

Lea rolls over to face him. "You owe me a graduation present." She kisses him passionately.

"As you wish." John gets up and flips the switch, leaving the room dark except the flickering of the movie. He slides under the blanket next to her. "Bed's still noisy though."

"We'll figure it out."

They begin kissing again, John runs his hand up her leg, encountering nothing beneath her pajama shirt. "Well then..."

"I think one of us is overdressed." Lea starts to push down his shorts. John takes over and strips from the waist down.

He resumes kissing her, pulling her nightshirt up. She stops him when he tries to remove it. He retreats, thinking she's changed her mind.

"No," she breathes trying to pull him back towards her, "it'll just be hard to explain if someone comes in and I'm completely naked. As long as it stays on, I can pull it back down real quick."

"Oh." Understanding, he resumes his caresses of her below her lifted, but still on, pajama shirt as she kisses his neck and nibbles at his earlobe.

Slowly and quietly John makes love to her, showering her in tender kisses and soft caresses. Afterwards, he holds her in his arms as she nuzzles into him and closes her weary eyes.

"John?" she whispers.

"Mm hmm."

"Can we do that again before you take me home?"

"Absolutely," John agrees matching her hushed tones and kissing her on the forehead.

"Hold up!" Jason's voice pulls Lea from her world of fanciful illusion. Her eyes, less responsive, remain closed.

Allie stops kissing him, "Shhh. Do you want her to wake up?"

Jason pushes her off him and points at the movie. "Play that back a little bit," he brings his volume back down to a hushed tone.

Emerald stretches, bending both ways at the waist, "What's going on?"

"I'm not sure yet, still listening," Raven answers.

"How 'bout I just ask?" Emerald drops her arms down and Lea opens her eyes just a sliver.

"No! They think I'm asleep, and I want to keep it that way." Raven protests, and Lea closes her eyes again.

"Why?" Emerald asks.

"Well, for one I think there was something going on while I was sleeping and for two I'm curious as to what's going on that they didn't want me to wake up for, so better to eavesdrop." Raven states her case.

"Okay, but I draw the line if it starts to repeat the car. Fair?" Emerald compromises.

"Fair." Raven resumes her reconnaissance.

Allie gets up and goes over to rewind the film. "What did you see? Where should I stop?"

"Right there, where Mr. Creepy starts talking to her. Now watch."

"What am I looking for?"

"Does she remind you of anyone?"

"Who did you have in mind?"

Raven doesn't hear a response because Jason silently points to Lea, still draped over the chair.

"Really?" Allie questions. "You think so?"

"Well, she isn't quite that heavy with the black make up, but.... Yeah!"

Allie watches the scene play out, her eyes squinted trying to see what Jason is referring to.

"Who are they talking about, Raven?" Emerald wonders, confused.

"I'm not sure, but I think they're talking about me. See why it's better if I let them think I'm still out?" Raven answers.

"Here... rebellious, defiant and laughing in his face. Tell me you haven't seen that in her." Jason points towards Lea again.

"Well, more so in this past year, I have," Allie is starting to see his point. "And she could totally wear a dress like that."

"You think? Her chest is much bigger than that though."

"Yeah, but she has no cleavage at all, so she can do something cut way down like that..., and she probably would if she thought she could get away with it without her parents having a cow."

Jason huffs and smiles to himself, trying to envision it.

"Oh!" Jason points at the screen excitedly, "This look right here when she asks if she can kill it herself. I have SEEN that look on Lea's face!"

Allie pulls her hand over her mouth, "So have I! I never noticed this before."

"Me either, that's why I had you go back to it."

"I love her to death, but she could be that manipulative and devious if she had to."

"Tell me about it," Jason agrees.

"Well, they're obviously talking about me," Emerald concedes. "Did they just insult me?"

"Maybe a little bit," Raven admits. "It all depends on if you view devious manipulation as a bad thing. Personally, I find it a very useful tool at times."

"Oh, so they were actually insulting you, not me," Emerald attempts to distance herself from the comments.

"Nice try, but that only flies if we were completely severed personalities, which we aren't." Raven destroys Emerald's justification.

Allie returns to the sofa with Jason. She leans back, lounging across the open side, gripping his shirt and pulling her to him. "You done with your comparisons now?" she asks coyly.

"Is she still out?" Jason goes along as she pulls on him, turning his head to make sure Lea hasn't awoken.

"Looks like it," Allie begins kissing his neck.

Jason closes his eyes, caving to the distraction, and setting aside his concerns that Lea could be faking it again.

"Oh, please, tell me this is not happening again," Emerald is disgusted.

"Yep, it's happening, but, on the flip side, it does explain that nasty look we got from Allie at the diner," Raven replies.

"She never told me she had a thing for Jason." Emerald is irritated by the omitted information.

"I'm not entirely sure she did before tonight, and I'm starting to wonder if there's some aphrodisiac in the air.

Everyone's running around with uncontrollable hormones."

"Would you be doing anything less if John was here?"

"But John and I have been together for how long? And he's not here, so it'd be nice if the cosmos would stop reminding me of that!"

"We might get that lucky, but it won't be tonight."

"Where's the happy bright side and rainbows, Emerald?"

"Flourishing shamelessly in my dreams for graduation."

Raven laughs heartily, "That they are."

"Can I, please, put an end to this auditory torment now?"

"Sure. I've had plenty enough of them slurping each other and sucking face."

Lea stirs slightly, setting off warning bells for the couple feverishly practicing their foreplay. Jason pops up, recomposing himself into a more innocent posture at the edge of the sofa. Allie rises slower and more disheveled.

Jason calls to her in a whisper, "Fix your hair!" Allie runs her hands over the tangled mess trying to smooth it back down on her head.

Lea stretches and yawns, slowly opening her eyes and deliberately giving them time to cover their tracks. "Where'd everyone go?"

"They took off after the first movie," Allie announced.

"First movie? What time is it?" Lea sits up, acutely aware that she needs to be heading home.

"Um, three-thirty-ish," Allie answers.

"Dude, we need to go," Lea focuses on Jason. "I need to get home."

"We were going to wake you as soon as the movie finished anyway," he says with a politician's honesty and charisma.

Lea raises her arms and tries to stretch out the knots and kinks. She reaches around the side of the chair blindly feeling for her shoes. Unable to find them, she looks over the edge. "Hmmm, they went farther than I thought." She stands and walks the three feet to collect her launched footwear. Allie chuckles at her.

Jason grabs Allie's knee while Lea's back is turned and winks. Allie blushes and grins. Lea grabs her bag of clothes, realizing it was a waste to have put forth the effort since she never bothered to change.

"Look at how wrinkled this dress is now," Emerald fusses.

"You can iron it after it gets washed," Raven scoffs. "If you think you can do it without burning a hole in it."

"Oooo, good point. Maybe Mom should do it." Emerald admits.

"That's what I thought," Raven mocks.

Lea heads out towards the door, knowing Jason is lagging behind.

"Who thought it was a good idea to have Prom during the spring. Hasn't it always been prime mating season?" Raven groans tartly.

"You weren't this sour last year and wouldn't be this year if the circumstances had been better." Emerald tries to sweeten her demeanor.

"You forget I was this sour last year," Raven corrects.

"No, you weren't." Emerald contradicts her.

"I spent the night with Kathy and HER date propositioned me right before we went to bed. Ring a bell?" Raven pours out the bitter memory.

"Oh yeah, that...," the recollection hits Emerald.

"Point, Game, Set, Match. Prom may have been the hope of young women to have an excuse to socialize with boys and not be wallflowers, but the timing was strategically placed for the most advantageous outcome of the male gender's alternately located brain," Raven ends her rant.

Jason and Allie meet Lea at the door. Allie hugs her, "Sorry it wasn't all you'd hoped."

"It's over, I'm alive, and you don't have to help me bury any bodies. I think that constitutes a success, all things considered." Lea hugs her back and walks out the door.

"Later," Jason waves at Allie as he follows Lea out.

Allie watches them get in the car and shuts the door.

~ *Clarifications and Cops* ~

Lea pulls out of the drive and waits for Jason to say something, anything. She reaches the entrance of the subdivision before she cracks and breaks the heavy silence. She puts the car in park in the middle of the deserted road.

"So we're going to sit right here until you start talkin'." She demands.

"What?" Jason feigns ignorance.

"If I get in trouble for being late, I'm blaming you."

"I don't know what you want me to say."

"Let's start with the fact that you're supposed to be dating Lauren and you're making out with Allie! Do you realize the position I'm in right now? Best friend one versus best friend two. If I tell Lauren, I betray Allie, and, if I keep my mouth shut, I'm not being loyal to Lauren! What the hell, Dude?"

"You were awake! I knew it!"

"Not the whole time."

"How much did you hear?"

"Enough. Not that it would have mattered if I had

been asleep the whole time."

"What do you mean by that?"

"I mean Allie has whisker burn all over her face, jacked up hair, and you have a hickey." She puts the car back in gear and pulls out onto the empty street. Jason laughs softly.

Lea continues, "I'm glad you find it funny. Think about this for a second. Monday at school, either everyone will figure out it was Allie, including Carl, OR they're going to think it was from me, and I'll toss you both in the fire before I let that rumor spread around and get back to John or his family."

"Oh. Yeah, it'll suck for Carl, but I'll make sure nobody thinks it was you."

"And Lauren? I realize she doesn't go to the same school , but it was still crappy to do to her. You just gonna avoid her 'til it's gone?"

"Won't have to. We went out a few times, but we aren't a couple. I don't even know when or if I'm going to see her again."

"But I thought you guys were an item."

"Nope. Why do you think I didn't care if she went with Brian tonight?"

"Well... I was told that it was because you had to work and couldn't take her yourself."

"Nah. We aren't that serious. By the way, I think there's a cop behind us. I saw him at the last intersection."

"I know. I saw him too. I take back some of the attitude. Thought you were a bigger jerk than you are."

"Why am I still a jerk?

"Um, how about snaking another guy's date? Isn't there some code about that sort of thing? Or maybe the fact that you did all that while her parents were asleep in the other room? Or, my personal favorite, you did it all while I was in the SAME room?"

"Okay, okay. I'll give you two out of three on that, but I'm not taking the hit about parents because if you sit there and tell me you've never done anything with parents in the house I'll know you're full of shit."

"Not my parents."

"And John's?" Jason pushes.

Lea blushes red thinking back on her recent dream and John's visit home.

"That's what I thought." he gloats.

"We aren't talking about me, and nobody else was in the room at the time."

"That might have pushed the boundaries a bit, but you didn't let us know you were awake either."

"What I heard was bad enough. I was afraid of what I might see if I opened my eyes."

This time it's Jason that is flushed, confirming Lea's suspicions that there is probably more that she doesn't need to know about, but also figuring Allie will offer her more details than she wants as soon as she realizes that Lea knows.

Lea continues, "You knew about my ride home. Allie doesn't, so I would have thought you would have shown more restraint. What is it with everyone humping like rabbits tonight?"

"Come on now. What do you really expect? I'm a teenage guy! A cute girl makes a move on me and my center of decision making hops on a bullet train and heads south. It's not like I get loads of offers and opportunities that I'm going to pass one up in hopes another one will come along."

Lea chuckles. This is what she likes about Jason, his candid honesty. "So she's the one that started it?"

"Guess you were asleep for that part…"

"I was."

"Just so I know how embarrassed you think I should be, which for the record, I'm not… How much did you hear?"

"Just the end."

Jason breathes a heavy sigh of relief as Lea pulls into the dark and emptied diner parking lot.

"You know it's your own fault," she adds. "You're the one that woke me up when you started comparing me to that chic in the movie."

"I KNEW IT!" Jason waves his finger pointing at her, grinning from ear to ear.

Lea pulls next to his car, "You really think I'm that dark and devious?"

"You can be…, but that's part of why we get along so well."

"I know I shouldn't ask this, but what are you planning to do about Allie now?"

"I don't know. Wasn't thinking about it like that, but, if she wants to repeat tonight, I won't turn her down." He smiles wide and raises his eyebrows before opening the door and hoping out. "Thanks for the lift. I don't know if it would have been as entertaining if we hadn't ridden together."

"Oh, great, nice way to make it my fault." Lea pops back at him before he can close the door. She makes sure his car starts, and they both drive away.

As she passes the back corner of the building, she notices a car with nothing but parking lights on that hadn't been there when they pulled in. She keeps an eye on it as they pull out on the road again. It turns its lights on and pulls out behind them.

"Hey Emerald, I thought you said they had better things to

do than following us all around giving us tickets." Raven draws her attention to the roller light bar across the top of the stalker car.

"I'm not doing anything wrong. Headlights are on, use turn signals, stay under the limit, but not too far under the limit. Have any of the bulbs burnt out?" Emerald nervously runs over her checklist.

Raven laughs at her, "Chill out. Everything's fine. I was only making you aware that they're there."

Lea follows Jason until she has to split off and turn towards her house. The cruiser continues following him, leaving her rearview in darkness. As she approaches the last stop before her home, she's met by another sheriff's car. She goes the last quarter mile and pulls into her driveway. She steps out of her car, and the cruiser turns on its lights, stopping in the middle of the vacant country road.

"Miss!" the officer behind the wheel calls her over.

She recognizes the gravelly voice as the older officer she had spoken to at the diner. She walks over to his car. "Yes, Sir."

"Just making sure you got home alright, young lady," he turns off the lights. "Did you enjoy the rest of your evening?"

"Truthfully, Sir, I slept through most of it. Woke up just in time to come home."

"Well, at least you stayed out of trouble."

"Yes, Sir."

"You better get inside and get some real sleep."

"Good night, Sir."

"Good Night, Miss."

Lea turns and walks to her house. The officer waits until she is safely inside and the door closes behind her before he heads down the street and back to his patrol.

She stops as she's passing by the dining table. She

173

reaches out to the saved flowers, lifts the vase, and breathes in the sweet fragrance. She had been so distracted when she got home earlier.

"I didn't even think to take care of them," Emerald holds a *flower in her hand.*

Raven soothes Emerald's guilt, "Don't be too hard on yourself. It'd been a nerve-racking night."

"Maybe, but they'd be dead if it'd been up to me."

"You can thank Mother in the morning."

Lea sets off for her room where she peels off her rumpled dress, throws on some comfy pajamas before washing her face and collapsing into her bed, succumbing to the complete mental exhaustion from the events of her day.

~ *Epilogue* ~

Lea is awakened by Vikki, phone in her hand.

"It's John," Vikki hands the phone over and walks out.

"Hello?" Lea answers, whispered and groggy.

"Hey there," the lilt in John's voice makes Lea smile.

"Hey… What time is it?'

"Apparently too early, Sleepyhead."

"Isn't it always too early for me?"

"A morning person you are not, but I waited 'til noon thinking it was safe."

"Really? I'm surprised they let me sleep this late."

"What time did you get in?"

"I little after four, I think."

"Seriously? Must have been a crazy night. How'd it go?"

"Don't ask."

"What do you mean don't ask? You were out 'til after four."

"That's the motto for last night. Don't ask."

"What happened?"

"Oh, I don't know. It's the one night of the year that every young person on the planet seems to act like a feral animal in heat, and you weren't here, but beyond that, it still pretty much sucked."

"I'm listening."

"You really want to hear all this?"

"Yep. All of it."

"Will the short version due?"

"Sure."

"Okay... So we get there and the seating is screwed up. I'm seated with percussion and rifles, which means Amanda Carter. I end up in the bathroom crying hysterically ready to go home before it even started. We got moved to an extra table. I didn't get to dance at all.

"Got stuck on the side of the highway when Dave's car broke. Allie told Mom she thought we were being drug searched because of the police car parked behind us. Scott and Rachel gave me a ride home and were doing who knows what in the front seat while I was pretending to sleep.

"Brian didn't meet us at the diner, so we didn't know where the after party was and ended up going over to Allie's instead for movies, where I fell asleep and she ended up making out with Jason, who is apparently not dating Lauren like I thought he was. Then I had a police escort home, and I poured myself into my bed trying to forget all of it until you called and woke me up asking about it."

"Oh... Eventful."

"Do you see now why my motto is 'don't ask'?"

"Yeah."

"So how are you doing?"

"Not bad. School's a little harder than I thought. I'm not doing bad, but I'm not doing as well as I need to either."

"What do mean?"

"It's like I'm getting low B's to high C's, but I need to be getting mid to high B's to pass."

"So what happens if you don't?"

"I wash out and get sent to a duty station without this specialty."

There's a long pause before Lea can think of something to say. "Just do your best. That's all anyone can ask of you. If you make it, great. If not, at least you tried."

"I am sorry I wasn't there last night, but I spent all day studying, and I'm going back for more extra study time later today.... Anything else going on?"

"I'm gonna talk to Mom about letting me stay out all night for graduation. The girls didn't have a curfew that night, so it's only fair that I shouldn't either. I was thinking we might hang out with Allie for a little bit and then if your parents didn't mind just spend the rest of the night hanging out at your house. Do you think they'd have a problem with that?"

"Probably not if I was gonna to be home?"

Raven and Emerald are suddenly very much awake and listening.

"You are not doing this to me, John... This is not how you're going to let my senior year end..." Raven rolls her eyes.

"So all that was a tradeoff for nothing?" Emerald is stunned.

Lea continues, "What do you mean 'IF you were going to be home'? You told me you weren't coming back for Prom because you wanted to be here for graduation instead."

"I know, but I really need to be here for the extra study sessions on the weekends."

Raven throws her arms in the air, "Un-freaking-believable!"

"So what exactly are you saying?" Lea asks.

John clears his throat, "I'm not going to be there."

Raven swoops her robes over the partially built enclosure. As they fall back into place, the walls are completed with reinforced steel, the door equipped with a locking mechanism the likes of which Emerald has never seen. Raven steps towards the door.

Emerald pleads with her, "Please, Raven, don't. You can't do this."

"I don't have much choice left. It's the perfect shield from abandonment. I'm on my own. If I don't look out for myself, there's nobody else that's going to do it for me. You know it as well as I do.

"We don't have that warm, close-knit, always looking out for each other type family. We had John, and now we don't, and I can't survive many more moments like this," *Raven raises her sleeve to show the gash she still bears from last night.*

"You're not just locking yourself away from the world. You're locking us all away, Raven."

"It's the only way I can continue to protect you..., protect Thistle..., protect myself." *With that Raven steps backwards into her small fortress and closes the door, changing Lea forever.*

Promedy of Errors

S. Weary

About the Author

S. Weary is a single mother of two, living in the Midwest, and not comfortable writing about herself. Just as Rose sees the missing details of Lea's life that she can't see herself, maybe it's better to get the true picture of who S. Weary is by how she is seen by those that are closest to her and best know her heart. They are unaltered, unpolished, real opinions from real people, so. if it's disjointed, please, understand.

Passionate. Compassionate. Loyal. -KS
S. Weary has the soul of a poet and a never quit spirit
that inspires all those around her. -DL
She is the most sweetest, caring, loving friend
anyone could ask for. -SS
She's a thoughtful, caring, charismatic spirited individual
with a sense of wonder and humor who is beautiful
even when she is in pain. -CB
S. Weary is a wonderfully maniacal, adventurous friend
who not only would bail you out of jail, but she would
be the friend sitting next to you in jail saying
'That was the best time ever.' -SM
A talented and inspiring woman who has the innate ability
to overcome obstacles and continue providing hope for
a bright future. -MJ
She has an amazing ability to see beyond peoples' masks into
their soul to their true beauty and the light that shines within
them and to hear what they are trying to say and express even
when they can't find the words for themselves or are too
afraid to step or speak beyond their defensive protections. -TS

Made in the USA
Lexington, KY
12 December 2013